TRUSTING THE TIGER

ZOE CHANT

ONE
TONI

TONI HAULED THE LAST SUITCASE OUT OF THE TRUNK OF her car and closed the lid with a satisfying *bang*. Behind her, the wooden cabin she had rented for the weekend cast a cool shadow over her battered Toyota Corolla. The rest of the campsite was bathed in brilliant sunlight. Beyond the cabins, mossy paths broke through the trees of the forest, leading who-knows-where.

Toni stretched and felt a smile begin to spread across her face. She'd been looking forward to this vacation for months, and she planned to make the most of it. A summer weekend in the great outdoors was just what she needed to de-stress from the endless grind of her life in the city. Toni's feet were already itching to start exploring the forest. She knew there was a river nearby, and an abandoned mine, as well as miles of hiking trails. Countless options for her to enjoy herself on her own.

Even if the original plan had been to enjoy it with her niece and nephew. Toni looked down at the pile of luggage by her feet and bit back a sigh. The twins had hopped out of the car the moment Toni had parked, and in the time it had taken her to test the key in the cabin door and pop the trunk, they had discovered that as well as a river, and an old mine, and all those hiking trails, Silver Forest also featured a BMX track, and was running a sports camp for kids over the weekend.

Toni had considered telling the twins they would have just as much fun hanging out with their aunt as they would racing around on bikes with a bunch of kids their own age. That thought had lasted all of half a second. She'd signed the permission slip and gotten started telling herself that she could have just as much fun hanging out on her own as she would have had spending the whole weekend with two ten-year-olds in tow.

First super fun solo activity? Unpacking the car!

And next up – *drumroll please*, Toni thought wryly – shoving everything in a corner of the cabin!

She sighed. There was no point trying to fool herself. Sure, it was a beautiful day, and she had a rare weekend of freedom ahead of her ... but she just couldn't shake off the feeling that every other person in Silver Forest had hightailed it the moment she arrived.

It sounded ridiculous, but it was ... kind of true. And one glance around the empty campsite only added fuel to the fire of her insecurities. The camp manager – Karen, her name was – had told Toni that all the other parents who had brought their kids to the camp had already headed out on their own adventure for the day, a bike ride into the foothills of the nearby mountains.

Karen had very kindly offered to loan Toni a bike if she wanted to join them. Toni had an immediate vision of a pack of lean, spandex-clad men and women skimming through the forest as light as leaves on the breeze ... and then of herself, lumbering up behind them. She didn't need to see Karen's stealthy up-and-down glance at her body to know she probably wasn't going to fit the mold for this group.

Toni was no stranger to feeling the odd one out. As the only full-time human in a family of cat shifters, she was used to feeling big and clumsy. Growing up with siblings who could naturally twist themselves into pretzels, or jump over her head, had left her feeling left out more than once.

Maybe that was why she was feeling so gloomy now. Being made to feel like she wasn't good enough, like her body wasn't powerful or flexible or fast enough, brought back those old feelings of loneliness.

She knew her family loved her, even if they left her in the dust athletics-wise. Just like she knew Lexi and Felix loved her, even if they sometimes found her less compelling than the possibility of crashing a BMX bike into a big pile of dirt. All the love in the world couldn't hide the fact that she would never be as gifted as the rest of her family.

Everyone else in the Oglietti clan had heightened senses, even in human form. They could identify different species of bird just by smell. Toni could barely identify most birds by sight.

Everyone else in her family could hold whole conversations in telepathic shifter-speak, sending their speech out to as many or as few people as they liked. Toni didn't have anywhere near that skill. The most she could manage was a sort of psychic shout – one that every shifter around her would hear, not just whoever she was talking to.

Everyone else in her family was a shifter. Toni was, essentially, human.

She would never measure up.

A bird whistled cheerfully above her head. Caught off-guard in the middle of her gloomy thoughts, Toni laughed. What was she thinking, worrying over things she could never change when the sun was shining and there was a whole forest to explore?

Toni heaved the last of the bags into the cabin and dusted off her hands. The paths at the edge of the campsite looked invitingly cool and shaded, full of the promise of adventure.

The sound of children whooping and yelling drifted through the trees. Toni grabbed a light sweater and water bottle and followed the noise. She would check what time the BMX activities finished for the day, and let the twins know she was going for a walk, before she headed off on her own.

She began to feel better the moment she stepped under the trees. Toni had always loved the outdoors, and now, the natural beauty of the forest seemed to wash her unhappy thoughts and insecurities away. Tall trees with leaves all shades of green swayed in the breeze, sending rippling sunlight across the ground. All around, summer flowers were peeking out, carpeting the woods with bright bursts of color.

This is what a real vacation should be like, she thought to herself. *Not worrying about what other people think, or stressing over whether the kids are enjoying themselves – just relaxing and taking some time for myself.*

Although it would be nice to have someone to share this with...

The path led out into a wide clearing, and Toni raised one hand to shield her eyes from the sun as she looked across it.

Then she jumped quickly backwards. Something shrieked past her at waist-height.

Toni blinked as the flash of movement resolved itself into a small child on an even smaller bike. Just as she was breathing a sigh of relief that she had avoided crashing straight into the kid, the bike tumbled off the side of the track into a bush.

"Hey! Are you all right?" Toni rushed forward. Before she made it halfway to the crash scene, the kid got to their feet, jumped back on the bike and rocketed off down the trail. Toni hadn't even had time to see whether the kid was a girl or a boy – just that they seemed to be mostly made out of mud. She winced slightly as she thought of what Lexi and Felix were going to look like by the end of the day.

"Don't worry about her. The smaller ones are pretty bouncy," called out a male voice. Toni turned to see a tall, broad-shouldered man walking toward her. With the sun behind him, she couldn't make out his features. "You, on the other hand, should probably get out of here."

Toni felt herself go red. Right. She *knew* she didn't belong here. She didn't need some rude stranger to pound the point home.

She was about to reply angrily when the man stepped forward.

"I mean – get out of the way!"

He reached out and grabbed Toni around the waist, swinging her to the side of the track just as two more cyclists raced around the corner. Then another one, and then lots more.

Toni didn't want to think what would have happened if she had still been standing in the middle of the trail when the cyclists swarmed past. Nothing good, she imagined. She would definitely be sporting some new tire-track bruises at least.

Instead ... the man was *definitely* still holding onto her.

As soon as she realized this, he let go, as though she'd spoken out loud. Toni mentally re-ran the last thirty seconds in her head. She was sure she hadn't said anything. Well, maybe squeaked a bit when the BMXers rushed past...

When you felt his strong arms around you, more like, a voice in her head teased. She ignored it.

"I'm sorry about that," the man was saying. "The trail from the cabins doesn't usually come out this close to the bike path, but they had to re-route after some trees fell down last winter. It's not a problem most of the time, but with this many kids..." He shrugged. "I think they get tunnel vision, and don't even think about whether someone might step out in front of them."

"Right," said Toni breathlessly. "People ... or bushes." She nodded at the bush the first cyclist had crashed into. Another pair of legs was sticking out of it, waving energetically. The man made a noise that was half-groan, half-laugh, and bounded over to help.

Making sure the man's attention was on the kid, not on her, Toni ran her hands down her shirt, smoothing the wrinkles from where he had grabbed her. She could still feel the heat of his arms around her. She had to force herself not to check if he'd left muscly-man-arm prints on her blouse.

And she could feel herself blushing. Not the angry red of a moment ago, either.

Her normal response to some strange guy grabbing her would be to slap him away, but even if this man hadn't just saved her from a tsunami of tiny BMXers...

Toni watched as her mysterious savior plucked the child

and bike from the bush, one in each arm, and set both upright on the path without breaking a sweat. She lingered over the view of his back and butt as he leaned down to check the kid wasn't hurt. His t-shirt had strained over his muscles, and she couldn't help but notice that his trousers were, well, well-fitted.

Toni realized her blush was going to stick around a while yet.

The young boy jumped on his bike again and disappeared around the corner. The man watched him go and then turned to Toni with a slight frown on his face.

"I should talk to Karen about this corner," he said. "That bush is only going to last so long as a buffer."

From this angle, instead of haloing his body, the sunlight lit him up, as though someone had set up a spotlight purely for Toni to enjoy the view. He must have been well over six feet tall, with dark russet hair curling over deep brown eyes. A thin, forest-green t-shirt stretched over a sculpted chest, and its sleeves rode up over his thick biceps. No wonder he had picked her up so easily – he looked like he was made of pure muscle, the sort you get from working hard with your hands all day, not popping steroids and veins in the gym.

Toni wasn't sure whether she wanted to thank him for pulling her out of the way, or rip him a new one for grabbing her instead of warning her about the danger. Instead, she huffed a small word best described as, *Umph*.

The man grinned at her and stepped back across the bike path. He was squinting slightly, and she realized that the sun was in his eyes when he tried to look at her. Just like it had gotten in hers before, when she was looking at him.

"I'm Jack Silver. Are you here for the BMX camp?"

"Sort of," Toni said. She tensed, waiting for the inevitable up-down glance and *are-you-sure-you-belong-here?* look. Then she frowned. "Wait – Silver ... as in Silver Forest?"

Jack laughed and ran his fingers through his dark red hair, looking away. Toni thought she saw a hint of pink appear on his cheeks and immediately regretted her question. The shock that had almost made her snap at him had drained away as fast as it had appeared. The last thing she wanted to do was embarrass the man who had saved her. But Jack didn't seem upset.

"Silver, as in ... oh, the forest, this camp, the old mine down the way, and I'm pretty sure Karen's got plans to name this BMX camp after me, as well. Seems like the sort of thing she would find funny."

He turned to walk further into the clearing, and Toni joined him.

Clearing was possibly too generous a word for the area. It was less thickly wooded than the forest itself, but there were still enough bushes and smaller trees around to keep Toni from being able to get a good bearing on where they were, or where any cyclists might pop out from.

No wildflowers would survive long under bike wheels, but the clearing, criss-crossed with bike paths, had a different sort of life to it. This part of the forest was full of the various sounds of small children enjoying themselves – laughter, whoops, and blood-curdling screeches. Toni tried to keep her eyes peeled for Lexi and Felix, but under their helmets and protective gear it was difficult to tell any of the kids apart.

"Watch out!"

Jack put out an arm to stop her from walking into two spinning wheels hurtling toward the ground. They had just rounded a patch of brush and come out next to a dirt-pile jump. Toni swore under her breath in a way that had become second nature after many adventures with the copy-cat twins: fiercely, but quietly enough not to be comprehensive to tiny ears.

She wasn't sure whether she was relieved or just depressed that human children could be as nerve-wracking as the shifter variety.

"You must have some sort of radar to know where they're going to jump out from," she joked. "I'm Toni, by the way. Toni Oglietti. I brought my niece and nephew out here for a weekend camping trip, but then they saw the sign for the BMX activities, and, well..." She waved abstractedly. "Here we are. Well, here *I* am, and there they are ... somewhere."

She clamped her mouth shut before she could babble anymore. What was wrong with her?

That was a silly question. She knew exactly what was wrong with her. The hottest guy she had ever seen had just saved her life. Well, saved her skin from a bunch of embarrassing bruises, at least.

She sneaked a look sideways and caught his eyes flickering away from her. Had she thought his eyes were brown? Maybe it was a trick of the light but they seemed gold-colored now.

She blinked, and his eyes were brown again.

It must have been a trick of the light. Toni had been amazed all day by how clear and bright the light was this far from the city. No exhaust fumes here, just the sweet smell of flowers and green growth.

I wish I could stay here forever, she thought wistfully, looking up at the wide blue sky. There wasn't a cloud in it—just endless blue, with the sun blazing white-gold in the middle.

"Oh, it might look nice now, but wait until winter and all of this will be frozen under six feet of snow and ice," Jack said absently.

Toni stiffened. Had she—? No, she was sure she hadn't said that out loud.

Jack must have caught the edge of her thoughts. That could happen with non-shifters sometimes, Toni knew. Toni had been the same before she had trained herself to hear and speak with her family in that way.

She needed to be more careful. It had been so long since she used mind-speak that she had gotten rusty at sharing and protecting her thoughts. It had taken her almost half the car ride here to re-learn how to think her thoughts *at* Lexi and Felix, rather than just let them bounce around her own brain. Clearly she had now gone too far in the other direction.

Toni sighed. Trust her to screw things up. After spending the whole drive out to the campground practicing mind-speak with the twins, she probably now needed to practice *not* mind-speaking.

"Do you live around here, then?" she asked lightly. No point drawing attention to anything strange.

Jack raised his eyebrows expressively. "That's right, the Silver man in the Silver house in the Silver Forest. That's me. It's a bit House-that-Jack-built, I know."

"Oh, come *on*," Toni teased. "You can't go and live in a *house* called Silver and then complain that everything's named after you. That's got to be on purpose."

He spread his hands innocently. "Oh, I suppose next you're going to say I could change my own name, too? Or just never have moved here?"

Toni laughed out loud. "What? You moved here? I

thought it must be an old family thing – come on, if you *chose* to be the Silver man in the Silver everything, that's all on you. What, did you move here just so you could complain about it?"

"You've got me!" Jack threw his head back and grinned up at the sky, his eyes shining. "My life is so terribly perfect, I have to seek out these embarrassments where I can. Every week, I order in a new set of silver cutlery just so I can complain when I unwrap it."

Toni's laughter escalated into an unladylike gurgle, which she hurriedly stifled.

They paused on the edge of another path to let another battalion of BMXers past. Toni tried to see if Lexi or Felix were among the group, but they all passed by so quickly she couldn't tell if they were there or not.

Like all the paths in the grounds, so many wheels had grooved the dirt that the track itself was almost a foot lower than the surrounding brush and walking trails. Jack held out his hand to help Toni across once the last of the bikers had sped away. Blushing – *again!* – she took it. His hand was warm, and large, the slight roughness of calluses brushing against her skin.

Toni licked her lips, trying to find something to say to distract herself from the feeling of his skin against her own.

"Is that what you do, then?" she joked. "Professional silverware-appraiser and gnasher of teeth?"

She closed her hand over itself as he let it go, holding on to the feeling of his fingers pressed against hers.

"Nothing so exciting, sorry. I'm – I guess you could say I'm in management. My company looks after a number of wildlife preserves around the world. Places that might otherwise be leveled for construction, no matter what sort of natural beauty would be destroyed."

"That sounds exciting to me," Toni said. "You must see so many amazing places. I'd love to see more of the world." Her mouth ran on ahead of her brain, which was still occupied by how hot the man walking beside her was. "This vacation is the farthest I've been from home in years, and it's only a half a day's drive from the city!"

Toni blushed. Why had she said that? Maybe her life wasn't the most exciting, but that wasn't the sort of thing you broadcast to hot guys you were trying to impress.

She sneaked a look sideways. Jack was smiling ruefully.

"You want to know the truth?" he said, gesturing to encompass the woods around them. "I've only been back here for a week, and this is already the most time I've spent in the outdoors in years. Turns out that being CEO means flying around the world to see the inside of a lot of conference rooms, and not much else." He chuckled. "The only time I get to actually *see* the parks my company looks after is if my assistant organizes a publicity shoot at one of them, and even that's just..."

His voice faded away. Toni could imagine what he was going to say. A photo shoot would mean being surrounded by a team of people, photographers, makeup artists, journalists – the opposite of the solitude of open spaces you wanted when you were exploring the wilderness.

"That sounds worse than never seeing the parks at all," she said, musing aloud. "All that wilderness to explore, and you're stuck in front of a camera all day."

"That's exactly it! And at the end of the day everyone hightails it to the nearest hotel. For more *meetings*."

Toni bit back a laugh. It was probably deliberate, but Jack sounded genuinely upset – and a little bewildered – that being successful had led to him being promoted out of his favorite part of the job.

"If you're in charge, can't you ... I don't know, de-promote yourself? Or give yourself a new job, one that requires lots of important looking at trees?"

Jack laughed. "Manager in charge of running off and hiding in the woods: got a nice ring to it, doesn't it?"

He paused, a question in his eyes. Toni sighed. Jack had pretty much bared his soul – she might as well do the same. Besides, it wasn't like she was ever going to see him again after this weekend. He would return to his hundreds of conference rooms, and she to her own daily grind.

She took a deep breath. Grumbly, but light-hearted – that was the tone to go for. The same tone he had used, though it was clear there was real emotion under his joking words.

"Please do the tactful thing and don't ask what *I* do for a living, or I'm going to have to reveal that I'm one of the pathetically underemployed, here babysitting her niece and nephew because my hours got axed so I'm free to play babysitter whenever Ellie and her husband are out of town." She made a show of looking around, as if sizing up the park. The sun was so bright it made her squint. "Hey, you don't need a live-in hermit for your forest here, do you? I'm sure I could find a suitable tree to live in. And you could ship me to one of your other campgrounds during those six-foot-snow winters. My rates are very reasonable," she continued as Jack dissolved into laughter.

The trees thinned out. Just ahead was a wide clearing, buzzing with activity. A few trucks and cars on the far side suggested there was a road somewhere. The area was dotted with picnic tables and, along one side, a series of packed-dirt jump ramps. No one was using the ramps at the moment, but Toni could imagine the chaos that would unfold when the group of BMXers returned.

"Here we are," Jack said. "The main control center. Chairs, drinks, and shade. Some of it's even not covered in mud."

Toni shaded her eyes. "No kids, though. What a shame, guess I'll have to sit down..."

"...and have a drink?" Jack finished. "I'll find you a chair – unless you'd prefer to start testing out a few trees?"

Toni giggled, unable to stop a delighted grin from lighting up her face. She sat down under a tree whose leafy branches cast a wide, cool shadow and watched Jack lope across the clearing. The "control center" he had pointed out was a truck with its trunk open to reveal a grill and a cooler of cold drinks.

Maybe, she let herself think, just maybe, this weekend wasn't going to be as bad as she had feared. Even if Jack disappeared back into the forest after this afternoon, the memory of those golden eyes would give the whole weekend a warm glow.

Well. His eyes, and ... other attributes. Toni enjoyed the view as Jack walked across to the truck, but quickly looked away as he turned back, drinks in hand. Her eyes stayed firmly on the trees, bike path, and everywhere else that wasn't his perfect pecs as he strolled back.

"Coke, or beer?" he asked, holding out two dripping wet cans. Toni took the soda and popped the tab.

"Thanks," she said gratefully. The sun was still high in the sky, and she was parched. *Because you've been panting over this guy so much*, her inner voice teased.

"Here's to freedom from meetings and retail jobs," she said, raising her drink. "Even if only for one weekend."

The air under the tree was cool, and its leaves cut out the harsh sunlight that had left them both squinting at each other as they crossed the maze of bike paths. As Jack sat down opposite Toni and raised his beer to her toast, she looked directly into his eyes for the first time, and he into hers.

Jack's whole body tensed. He dropped his drink on the ground.

"Are you all right?" Toni leaned forward and put a hand on Jack's arm. His muscles were so tense they were jumping under his skin. His whole body was shaking. She looked into his face. His eyes were rings of gold, almost drowned by his huge, black pupils.

"I – oh, shit," he muttered roughly, and broke her gaze. He passed one hand over his face, ruffling his hair. "I'm sorry, I – I have to go. Excuse me." He rose suddenly, kicking his can in his rush to get away. Beer splashed out onto the dry dirt.

Toni stared after him, shocked. What had happened? Had she said something—?

No, she realized dismally as she followed Jack's unsteady flight away from her. He was running so fast he practically collided with a blonde woman. Toni recognized her from earlier that day: Karen, the woman who had organized the BMX tournament.

Karen was petite and toned; her long blonde hair, pulled back in a perfect ponytail, shone like gold as it caught the sun. She was everything that Toni wasn't.

A lump of sour unhappiness lodged in Toni's stomach. It

was clear as crystal what had happened. Big, ungainly Toni Oglietti would always come second best to someone like Karen.

Toni realized she was gripping her drink so hard the aluminum can was buckling. She took a deep breath and forced herself to relax. She'd met guys like Jack before. He probably hadn't even been flirting with her, just being friendly. And if he dropped her like a hot potato the minute someone he liked better came along ... well, yeah, that hurt. It hurt a lot. But it wasn't like she would ever see him again.

It's just like all those assholes who come into the shop looking for someone to bitch at, she told herself. *It says more about them than it does about you.*

Toni had just managed to make herself feel, if not entirely better, then at least not totally miserable, when a shriek cut through the air.

"Auntie Toni! Auntie Toni, watch me-e-e-e-e!"

Toni's new-found calm went flying. She looked up and automatically flinched as a bicycle whizzed past her. Lexi, barely recognizable under her safety gear and a thick layer of mud, raced at top speed toward one of the jump ramps.

Toni closed her eyes tightly. One of the many things she had not inherited from her family was their ability to enjoy acrobatic feats of insanity without being terrified someone was going to get hurt. She couldn't even watch Lexi take the jump without feeling sick to her stomach.

A small hand plucked at her elbow. *<Hello>* whispered a soft voice in her mind – Felix. Then he said out loud, "You can look now, Auntie Toni!"

Toni opened her eyes just in time to see Lexi hanging upside-down six feet in the air. Her stomach flipped as the slight figure sped earthward, somehow twisted right-side-up, and hit the dirt wheels-first in a skid of pebbles.

She shut her eyes again. "Thanks, Felix. Your sense of timing is just so, so great."

Felix flung his arms around Toni's shoulders. "Come on-n-n!" He giggled. "You know we have to trick you, or you'll never watch us do *anything*."

<Besides> he added, *<You know we're never going to actually get hurt. Bikes are* way *easy.>*"

Toni sighed, but she couldn't argue with that. As cat shifters, Felix and Lexi were almost magically athletic. Like everyone else in Toni's family, the two of them had grown up with perfect control of their shifter and human bodies. So, as dangerous as the BMX tricks looked, Toni logically knew they weren't in any danger.

Not that any of that stopped her from silently freaking out when they jumped into activities like the BMX aerials. Logic took a back seat to what Toni liked to think of as "Auntie terror," i.e., the fear of what her sister would do to her if anything happened to her children while Toni was looking after them.

Felix tugged at her sleeve and pointed across the track. "Look! There's Karen! She's awesome. She showed me how to do a new jump."

Toni followed Felix's pointing arm to where Jack was still talking with the slim blonde woman. Jack turned away just as she looked across, putting his back to her.

Karen was looking up at him, her hair a cascade of perfectly, straight, perfectly shiny gold. Toni looked away, disappointment curling in her stomach.

"I'm going to try it that new jump now!" Felix crowed, jumping on his bike and wheeling across to the ramp.

"And I'm not going to watch!" Toni caroled after him, secretly grateful for the distraction.

Toni settled back to watch Felix as he launched himself back onto his bike. She steeled herself as he approached the jumps. *This is fine,* she told herself. *I didn't actually scream out loud when I watched Lexi jump. I can totally deal with this.*

Besides, the more I freak out over the kids, the less I'll think about Mr. Perfect Butt over there.

"Watch *this!*" Felix yelled, and Toni flinched as he twisted around to poke his tongue out at her. He swerved toward a tree, over-corrected in the other direction, and then righted himself at the last second, cackling madly. Toni hadn't even had time to leap to her feet.

<*Made you look!*> Felix's voice echoed in her head. Toni could rarely tell when her shifter family were using their telepathic voices rather than their real ones, but she could tell this time. The clue was that there was no way he could have called out to her like that with his tongue still sticking out.

Toni rolled her eyes and slumped back in her chair. If she was ever going to get used to her niece and nephew's death-defying displays, now was the time.

With the late afternoon sun behind her, the whole clearing was flooded in clear, golden light—the perfect calm backdrop for her niece and nephew to go wild.

Lexi was hollering encouragement at Felix as he sped toward a ramp. Toni had just taken a gulp of soda and fixed her eyes determinedly on the small figure hurtling across the ground when the shade of the tree suddenly got a lot colder.

The crunch of leaves told Toni someone had stepped up behind her.

For one crazy moment, Toni thought it might be Jack, come back to apologize for running off. But a glance across the clearing showed her he was still deep in conversation with Karen.

She twisted in her seat to look at the stranger, and frowned. It was a man – and, whoever he was, he had crept up way closer than she'd thought. Toni fought a sudden impulse to back away.

"Uh, can I help you?" she asked.

He was tall – not as tall as Jack (why did her stupid brain keep going back to him? Ugh!) – but tall enough that he loomed over Toni in her chair. She supposed he was good-looking, but it was a sleek, unnatural handsomeness, like he'd been buffed and polished in a workshop before being let outside.

He was holding a tablet of some sort in his hand, and seemed more interested in it than in answering her question. Toni glared, and shivered. The whole forest to stand in, and not only did he choose to creep up behind her, but now he wasn't even going to acknowledge her?

Silver Forest? she thought grumpily. *More like Forest of Asshole Men.*

Well, she was pissed off enough not to let him just stand there ignoring her.

"Hello?" she said, unable to keep the sarcasm out of her voice. "Anyone there?"

She waved a hand in front of him. He tucked the tablet under one arm and, like someone had flicked a switch, suddenly looked down at her with a gleaming smile on his face.

"Andre de Jager," he said smoothly, plucking her hand out of the air and shaking it. "Sorry, I was just – checking something."

Toni couldn't pick his accent; it was slightly foreign, but not one she could recognize. Maybe something European, or South African?

"Toni Oglietti," she replied shortly, unwilling to let his sudden show of manners make up for his lack of them before. "Do you mind? You're—"

She paused. It wouldn't make sense for her to say, "You're blocking my sun," because she was already sitting in the shade of the tree. But she couldn't shake the sense that the air had grown colder the moment he turned up.

"...standing behind you like a particularly creepy shadow. I do apologize." He moved in front of her – but without letting go of her hand.

"Right." She pulled her hand away. "And that was an extremely creepy ... pirouette ... thing."

"Then I apologize again. What a bad first impression I'm making. And on one of Jack's ... friends, no less."

He was still smiling, but Toni had worked retail long enough to know when someone was making nice.

"You know Jack?" she asked.

"Oh, we go a long, long way back," Andre said, and laughed unpleasantly. That is, his laugh sounded entirely normal – even pleasant – but it somehow ... wasn't.

It was hard to concentrate on talking. Her heart was hammering in her chest, a panicked drumbeat telling her *danger–danger–danger*. Her eyes flicked automatically to

Felix and Lexi, who were playing happily on the other side of the clearing with the other children.

Was it her imagination, or did the stranger – de Jager – follow her gaze?

What was going on? Why was this guy freaking her out so badly? All he'd done was turn up and be a bit of a dick. So why was her body going to panic mode?

Toni shook her head to clear it. She was being irrational. She was just tired, probably. She'd driven all the way from the city today, and it was so hot, and Jack had dropped her like a hot potato *not that she cared* ... yeah, she was probably just tired.

And now she'd snapped at this guy for basically nothing. Toni rubbed her face and started to stand up.

"Look, I'm really sorry, but I've got to..." *got to go, got to clear my head, got to have a nap like a freaking five-year-old who's gotten over-excited* ... Toni's head buzzed as she tried to think of an excuse to leave.

She stumbled into Andre as she stood up, and he dropped the tablet. Automatically, Toni stooped to grab it before it hit the ground. As her fingers closed around the black plastic shell, a shock like electricity arced up her arm.

"Ouch!" she yelped, and let go of the device. It fell to the ground and lay there, blinking.

Toni sucked on her stinging fingers and stared at the thing. Now that she could see it clearly, it didn't look like a tablet after all. The screen and interface didn't look like machine she'd even seen – plus, it felt like it had *bitten* her. What the hell?

"Shit, that really hurt!"

TWO
JACK

Karen was saying something. Several somethings. Actually she had been speaking constantly for the last ten minutes, but Jack hadn't picked up a word of it, because every atom of his attention was focused on another woman.

Toni.

He knew exactly where she was, still sitting under the tree, less than a hundred yards away. He didn't need to turn around to see her; her image was front and center in his mind's eye. That mane of dark brown hair, almost black, wild curls escaping from their loose ponytail to frame her sweet round face. Her sparkling eyes, blue as the morning sky, and the way she'd glanced up sideways at him from under her long, thick lashes.

Jack closed his eyes briefly, remembering her plump, red lips. And below all of that ... he almost moaned aloud in frustration at the memory of her body, held close against his. Her soft, generous curves. The heat of her body and that tantalizing blush as she felt his own heat...

And then – those same blue eyes losing their brightness, barely able to look at him. That mobile mouth turning down, lips tucked in at the corners, biting down on her feelings. She had looked that unhappy when he first saw her, trapped in her own unhappy thoughts. He had brought her out of herself, teased out those flirtatious, flashing eyes and open smile – and then slammed the door in her face.

His life had changed in less time than it took him to draw a breath, and the first thing he did with that breath was ruin it. The best thing that had ever happened to him, and like an idiot, he'd thrown it away.

He'd been attracted to Toni the moment he first saw her. With those curves, and that face, how could he not be? As they had talked, he had realized she felt the same attraction, but it wasn't until they locked eyes for the first time that he understood the truth. What she was. *Who* she was.

He'd thought she was just a stunning human woman. Someone he would have loved to get to know better but who, in the end, would just be a harmless summer fling. After the last few months, he'd welcomed the thought of summer romance, even a brief one. He'd felt happy, lucky, like everything was going his way. Then – *bam*.

As soon as he looked into her eyes properly, he knew.

She was his mate.

He couldn't deny it. He literally couldn't even consider denying it. His brain leapt away from the thought like it was poison. The moment he had looked into her eyes, and seen her looking into his, he had known. Certainty had struck his body like a bolt of lightning. His tiger, already close to the surface out here in the wilderness, had risen up and purred in delight.

It had been all he could do not to tear her clothes off then and there.

Instead, he had panicked. Turned away.

Abandoned her.

What else could he do? He was a shifter, his human self inextricably bound up with his tiger self. And she was a human. He'd heard of shifters pairing up with humans before, hiding their true selves, but he'd never heard of it working out in the end.

After all, what would she say if he told her his secret: that he could transform into a massive tiger? That the tiger was a part of him? She would think he was crazy. And if he did shift in front of her, he would be lucky if she didn't run away screaming.

Jack sighed. He had thought it was his lucky day, but of course it would turn out to be just his same old bad luck. It was true what he had told Toni. His job had taken him all over the world. But that wasn't the whole truth.

His main mission had been to extend his trust's land holdings – keeping vital habitats safe and untouched for local wildlife – but in the back of his mind all that time he had hoped he might find *her* on his travels. His one. His mate.

God knows he had looked. For ten years, Jack had introduced himself to shifter clans the world over, from a caribou shifter tribe in the north to a small colony of penguin shifters in icy Antarctica. He must have met every eligible shifter woman from here to Timbuktu. And now, after he had finally given up hope that there was a woman out there meant for him...

A human. A perfect, beautiful, funny human. So now his

choice was between being with his mate, but never being *himself* with her – or staying alone.

Jack had fuzzy childhood memories of asking his parents about how they met, what it was like. They had told him that finding your mate was meant to be like finding a missing part of yourself, but how could that happen if he had to hide part of himself to be with her? And could she really be happy with someone who couldn't trust her with his whole self?

"...you're not listening to a thing I'm saying, are you?" Karen snapped her fingers in front of Jack's eyes. "Wakey, wakey, big fella."

He blinked. "No, I was..."

Karen snorted. "Don't try telling me you were listening. I just said 'You're not listening to a thing I'm saying' about ten times before you clicked. You were miles away."

"Not *miles* away," Jack admitted gruffly.

Karen was one of his oldest friends. Jack had bought the land around the old Silver mine ten years ago – one of his earliest projects with the trust – and she had stuck to him ever since, like a leggy blonde burr. And not in a romantic way. It turned out that she had been bringing classes from underprivileged schools out here on the sly for camping trips for the past several years, and was adamant she be allowed to keep doing so, preferably with some official funding.

Jack had been happy to set aside some of the land for a proper camping and recreation ground. As well as being a refuge for wildlife, the park would be a place for children to learn about the land. A place of knowledge, and learning. And, sometimes, BMXing.

Jack forced himself back to the present. Karen was looking past him, back across the picnic area.

"Not 'miles away,' huh?" she said dryly. "I thought you came stampeding over to me a bit faster than usual. Don't act too coy, though. It looks like you're not the only competitor in the field."

Jack spun around, his tiger roaring inside him, teeth bared. He wasn't a jealous guy – at least, he had never been a jealous guy before now – but the hairs on his arms prickled as he looked across at Toni and the man standing over her.

His first impulse was to storm over there and tell the guy where to go. He held himself back. He didn't have any claim over Toni, particularly if he was deciding to ignore the mate bond and stay out of her life. He had no right to get angry over other men talking to her.

There was a sudden movement; as Jack watched, his shifter eyes picking up every detail, something slipped from the man's grip and fell to the ground. Jack had the strange feeling that whatever-it-was had been dropped deliberately, but the thought had barely crossed his mind when Toni bent to catch the object, and then dropped it with a cry, as though it had stung her.

She cradled her hand, pain flitting across her face.

Jack didn't hesitate any longer. He covered the distance between then in a handful of long strides. Closer, he could clearly see the discomfort in Toni's face and stance. It wasn't just her injured hand; his tiger's senses, more attuned than his human ones, zeroed in on her tightened nostrils, fast breathing and the tense muscles in her neck. She was more than just uncomfortable. She was on the edge of panic.

Toni's eyes jerked toward him as he approached and filled with an unmistakable look of relief. That was all the invitation he needed.

Jack stepped in beside Toni, sliding one arm behind her to rest reassuringly on her lower back. He felt her lean backwards into him, almost unnoticeably, the slightest pressure on his hand.

"Everything okay here?" he said calmly, though every muscle in his body was coiled to strike.

The man was glaring bullets at Jack. A faint memory stirred in the back of Jack's mind. Had he met this guy before?

"That thing *shocked* me," Toni snapped at the stranger.

The man smiled, a smooth, easy expression that Jack didn't trust an inch. "As I was saying before we were interrupted, Toni, it must have been static electricity—"

"Oh, come on," Toni scoffed. "Static electricity? I've got a niece and a nephew who're both obsessed with pranking each other. Trust me, I know what static electricity feels like. It doesn't hurt that much, and it sure as hell doesn't leave a mark."

She held out her hand. The tips of her middle and index fingers were an angry red, as though they had been burned.

Jack felt a growl start to build in his chest.

The stranger either didn't notice Jack's rising anger, or didn't care. He looked at Toni's fingers and an entirely unconvincing expression of sympathy arranged itself on his face.

"Oh, dear. I've a first-aid kit back with the rest of my gear, Toni, if you'll follow me..."

"We've got plenty of medical supplies back at the truck," Jack interrupted, almost spitting the words. "She doesn't need to follow you anywhere."

Jack stepped forward, his arm still curved protectively around Toni. He topped the other man by over a head. It wasn't hard to stare him down when he was literally *staring down* at him, though he would have much preferred to straight-up stamp him into the dirt.

His tiger was spoiling for a fight – and not just his tiger. This was one thing both halves of him agreed on.

Come on, you bastard, talk back. Give me one reason to knock you down.

The enraging, vapid smile returned to the man's face. "I guess I'll just see you around the camp, then."

"Guess again," Toni said crisply, before Jack could get a word in. "You – oh, just *go away*, would you," she finished, her voice trembling. Jack could feel her body still slightly shaking against his.

The other man still seemed oblivious to the antipathy both she and Jack felt for him. "Until we meet again, then," he said mildly, and set off slowly.

Toni raised one hand to his retreating back. "An apology would be nice!" she yelled, to no response. They both watched silently as he disappeared between the trees.

Jack felt Toni droop, tension leaving her body in a rush. "Oh, what the *hell* was that about?" she stormed, and turned to him with her eyes blazing. "I don't think much of your friends, Jack."

"Who, that guy? I've never seen him before in my life." Jack paused, that faint memory flickering again. "At least ... I don't think..."

Toni glared. "He said his name's Andre de Jager. And that you and he go way back."

De Jager...

Images flashed in Jack's mind as memories he'd tried to forget rose to the surface. Wide, empty tundra. The hot, hot sun of South Africa. Weeks spent negotiating with local authorities. And then, mere hours before the conservation pledge was to be signed...

Blood pooled on the ground, sticky and red. Flies already buzzing in hordes over the bodies, and the stench of death thick in the air.

A group of local rich kids had objected to the conservation agreement. De Jager was the ringleader, a spoiled, entitled prick who thought the only good thing about the wilderness was that it was full of creatures he could kill. Faced with the ban on all hunting in the region, he and his friends had decided to see the season out with wholesale slaughter.

They'd piled their trophies directly in front of the governer's house where the agreement was being signed. Jack had walked out of what was meant to be his first big success for the trust, straight into a vision from hell.

And now, ten years later, de Jager was here. Why?

"You do know him," Toni accused, her eyes narrowing.

"Yes. But he's not a friend. Not even close." Quickly, Jack explained how he knew de Jager, and what the man had done. Toni's expression went from suspicious to horrified.

"But what's he doing here? It's not hunting season," she said, astounded. "There's no big game in the park anyway, is there?"

"No big game," Jack agreed, "and no hunting, period. This whole place is a nature preserve."

"You don't think this could be some sort of revenge thing, do you?" Toni suggested cautiously.

Jack shrugged. "It's been ten years, and he hasn't caused any trouble at the preserve in South Africa in all that time. He was just a kid back then, and you know, people do change."

He didn't believe what he was saying himself, and Toni was shaking her head slowly.

"No ... he seemed ... wrong." She shivered, and Jack saw her eyes flicker across to the jump ramps. Two dark-haired, blue-eyed children, a boy and a girl, were egging each other on under Karen's amused supervision. *They must be Toni's niece and nephew*, he realized. And de Jager had freaked her out badly enough that she was worried about them.

A sudden protective urge rose up in him. Whatever reason de Jager had for coming here, Jack would deal with it, but he wouldn't put up with his frightening Toni and her family.

"I'll make sure the park rangers are on the lookout for him," he said aloud. "And that they're to throw him out on sight. If he wants to see me, he can make an appointment through my EA, like everyone else."

Toni cracked a weak smile. "He must be bad, if you're willing to plan a work meeting to get him out of your hair."

She hugged herself, looking so anxious and miserable even through her brave smile that Jack couldn't hold himself back anymore. He wanted more than anything to gather her in his arms right then and there, sweep her away to his house deep in the forest, keep her safe – anything to banish that hunted look from her eyes.

He was under no illusions that sweeping Toni off her feet right now would more be more likely to scare her than comfort her. He made up his mind.

"Look," he began, stumbling over his words. "I'm really sorry about all this. This is meant to be your weekend getaway, and instead ... well, it doesn't seem like you're having a great time. And you should be. Let me make it up to you."

"Well, you got me a drink," Toni replied with a straight

face. They both looked down to where her Coke lay spilled on the ground, next to Jack's beer.

"Right. And then I ran off and left you to be stalked by a weirdo from my past. So I owe you twice," Jack offered.

"Maybe three times, if you count organizing this BMX thing that has stolen Felix and Lexi's sporty little hearts," Toni added.

"Two and a half," Jack countered. "I provided the campground, but Karen's one-hundred-percent to blame for the bikes."

"Deal." A smile – a real one, this time – twitched at the corner of her mouth, and she held out one hand. "Shake on it?"

They shook, both giving the action the mock seriousness it deserved.

"First things first, let's get you to that first-aid station," Jack decided. "Your fingers – hang on, was it the other hand?"

Toni stared at her fingers. "No, it was definitely this hand..." She flexed her fingers experimentally. "Wow, the marks have faded really fast."

"Does it still hurt?"

"No, it's ... fine." She frowned. "Weird."

Jack gently took her hand and examined it. Five minutes ago, her fingertips had been a painful-looking red, as though she had touched a hotplate, but now there was no sign anything had ever been wrong. Toni's fingers were unharmed, soft, delicate, and as beautiful as the rest of her.

With his shifter senses, Jack felt Toni's heartbeat quicken. Her fingers started to curl around his own, and then she pulled back self-consciously.

Jack's own body was responding to her excitement. He

coughed, willing himself to calm down. Then inspiration struck.

"I've got it. With your niece and nephew up to their eyeballs in dirt bikes, your plans for the weekend are probably shot, right?" He took in her glum nod. "Then let me make it up to you. How do you feel about joining me on a picnic tomorrow?"

Toni looked up at him, and the tentative hope in her eyes made his heart swell in his chest.

"I'd ... I'd like that," she said, the words tripping over each other. "I'd *really* like that."

The sun had crept toward the horizon as they talked, so Jack offered to help herd the twins back to the cabins once the bikes were packed away for the day. Lexi and Felix – he made a mental note to ask Toni about the names – hardly touched the ground the whole way back to the camping ground. They clambered up trees and jumped across rock piles. He couldn't help but think that Toni would hardly have had a relaxing weekend if she had to look after the two of them the whole time. He left them madly waving to him from the cabin door, and turned to start the long walk through the trees to his own home.

There was no sign of de Jager, but then he had stalked off in the opposite direction to the cabins. If he was staying in the campground, he must have his own tent somewhere off the beaten track. He hadn't been lying when he told Toni he doubted de Jager was up to anything, but even so, knowing how much the man had unnerved her, he pulled out his phone and rang the head ranger to let him know bad news was skulking around.

THREE
TONI

"You two are *FILTHY*," Toni grumbled as Lexi and Felix stripped off their sweaters to reveal sub-strata of dirt. "Right, grab your shower kits, and let's get to the showers before everyone else descends on them."

"Not gonna!" crowed Lexi. Before Toni could so much as *tssk* the small girl began to shrink and twist inside her clothes. Her sleek brown hair shrank down and then seemed to stream across her skin. Moments later a lithe, chocolate-brown Burmese kitten wriggled out from the pile of clothing. Lexi the human might have been covered in muck, but Lexi the cat was spotless, her fur gleaming. She stretched out one paw and licked it smugly. <*See? No need to shower. I just leave the dirt behind!*>

"You mean you leave it all over the floor." Toni sighed. Her eyes had automatically flicked to the window as Lexi began to shift, checking that the curtains were safely drawn and no one could see in.

She picked up the pile of clothes, shook the loose dirt from them, and then started to hunt around for a broom to sweep the mess out the door. "Felix, why don't we..."

Too late. Out of the corner of her eye she saw Felix drop to the floor, but the cat that emerged from this pile of clothing was far less sleek than his sister. While Lexi had managed to shift out of her coating of dirt as well as her clothes, Felix wasn't so lucky.

"Oh, Felix." She sighed sympathetically. "Do *not* try to lick that all off yourself, you'll make yourself sick. Come here. I'll brush you down."

He meekly jumped on her lap as she sat down with the brush. Toni secretly suspected that the boy could shift as well as her sister, but he liked being brushed more than he liked showing off. Lexi prowled around the room as Toni groomed dirt out of her brother's hair.

Toni kept finding herself glancing nervously at the door. She was still on edge from her encounter with de Jager earlier, and Jack's story about how he had deliberately hunted down all those soon-to-be-protected animals in Africa had only added to her bad feelings.

She shivered. Poor Jack. That event must have happened pretty early on in his career. To have someone deliberately, savagely sabotage your life's work like that ... it must have been horrific. But he had kept going. He hadn't let de Jager scare him away from his passion.

Toni straightened her shoulders. *She* wouldn't let de Jager get to her, either. Screw him. Anyway, she had far nicer things to think about. Things like...

Her mind instantly drifted back to Jack Silver. In less than half an hour, Jack had charmed her, deserted her, and come to her rescue. She was still confused, and a little hurt, by how he had run off, but the way he had come back to defend her the moment that creep had cornered her ... it made her heart flutter.

He had been so concerned for her safety, and the children's. Where even the thought of de Jager sent a shudder down her spine, thinking about Jack made a warm glow spread through her whole body. And ever since they had parted, in every spare moment her mind had started drifting back to memories of his eyes, his lips, his body – actually, *drifting* was a poor word for it. It was more like he was a whirlpool, and she was caught in the current. Even when they had been discussing that monster de Jager, she had felt her body leaning in to Jack, as though magnetically attracted.

Toni sighed. It had been so long since she last had a boyfriend, her body was clearly going into crush overdrive. And maybe that wasn't a bad thing. Maybe a little picnic-based flirting was just what she needed.

Jack might be more interested in her as a worried park guest than a potential fling, but spending time with him would hardly be a chore. And the way he had reacted to de Jager that afternoon, if he turned up to make trouble, Jack would soon run him off.

Tomorrow was going to be a good day. She knew it. Well ... she *hoped* it. Very strongly.

The dirt covering Felix was fairly dry, so it didn't take her long to brush it out of his short hair, even if he did complain every time she had to roughly work out a knot. At last she stood up and grabbed the broom to sweep the mess out the door.

"All right, kittens, bedtime. You can sleep cat-form if you like, but we've got to make up your sleeping bags so it looks kosher if someone comes and knocks on the door – hey! Come back here!"

Two dark-brown streaks blurred out the door before she could shut it. Oh, damn, damn, *damn*. Those stupid kids – what if...

Shifters were secret. That was the number-one rule, the prime directive. You don't let humans know shifters exist, you don't let humans know *you're* a shifter, and you *definitely* don't shift in front of them.

And there were reasons for that. The sort of reasons that made the bottom fall out of Toni's stomach as she grabbed a flashlight and darted out after the twins.

Thank god we've got the last cabin in the row, Toni thought as she stepped under the trees. Leaving the flashlight off, she waited impatiently for her eyes to adjust to the darkness.

Tiny, reflective eyes caught the crack of light that shone out through their cabin's curtains. Tiny, reflective eyes ... halfway up a tree.

"Come back down here!" Toni hissed. "You know what your mom and dad said! You can't behave here like you can back home!"

<Catch me first!> Lexi scrambled higher and Toni gritted her teeth.

As if. At least with Lexi she knew it was just a matter of waiting. Felix might not be able to shift as tidily as his sister but he was a far more confident climber. She watched as Lexi jumped and scrambled her way to a higher branch. All she had to do was wait, and make sure she was underneath when Lexi decided she wanted to jump down.

"Felix? Felix, I swear, if you get more mud on yourself I will dump you in a tub and *scrub* you," she muttered darkly.

There was no response. Toni shut her eyes and concentrated.

<KIDS. EITHER YOU *BOTH* COME BACK HERE, RIGHT NOW, OR WE LEAVE *FIRST THING* TOMORROW MORNING.>

Mind-speaking was a strain, but it was a more effective way of getting through kitten-brains than human speech. After a few moments a tiny dark shadow separated itself from the trunk of the tree and clawed at Toni's knees to be picked up.

<*Hello, Felix. Lexi? What about you?*>

<*But nothing's going to* happen> Lexi whined. <*Mom and Dad would let us...*>

"You know that's not true," Toni replied firmly. Ellie and Werther were loving, paranoid parents. They'd heard enough stories about shifters going missing to let their kids shift anywhere but the safety of their own home. Toni was already risking sisterly wrath by letting the kids shift in the cabin in the first place, but now...

<*And ... I'm stuck...*> Lexi admitted in a tiny voice.

Toni sighed. "Just jump," she whispered. "I'll catch you."

She held out her arms and grabbed her niece as she flung herself sulkily out of the tree. Both kittens firmly clutched in her arms, she went back to the cabin, carefully closing the door and curtains before Lexi and Felix transformed again.

Both of the twins decided to sleep in human form. Toni was

not-so-secretly relieved. She tried to call her sister's cell so the kids could say goodnight to their parents before they went to sleep, but it went straight to voicemail. Toni could feel herself gearing up to admit to her sister that she'd let the twins shift – and go outside! – and in her panic to *not* talk about that, ended up babbling to the machine about creepy big game hunters. She hung up, feeling like the most irresponsible sister in the world.

Surely she could handle one more night of this. The twins might be kitten-brained, but they weren't stupid enough to transform while they were on the BMX course tomorrow. She could spend the day relaxing – with Jack...

Visions floated through her mind. Her and Jack, walking through the sun-speckled forest. Eating their lunch by the side of a lake. In her imagination, she didn't get sweaty in the summer heat, and no ants made their way into the sandwiches. He would be wearing another tight t-shirt, and she would be wearing...

Okay. That could be a problem.

Toni thrust her cell at Felix as she rummaged through her pack. "Try your parents again, will you? And if you can't get through, leave a message telling them goodnight. I'm sure your mom will get it."

She waited another moment, frowning down at her selection of shirts, and then raised one warning finger. "I said 'try your parents,' not 'play Angry Birds,' Felix."

"Aww..." she heard Felix moan as the tinny music turned off.

All the rummaging in the world wouldn't change the fact that she had packed for a casual-to-schlubby weekend of camping. There was nothing in Toni's pack that was even

close to what she would normally wear for a – well, it wasn't a
date, precisely. It was a...

...hot man playing her personal bodyguard to apologize for
a creepy guy annoying her?

Toni wasn't sure there was a word for that.

She settled on a light blue wraparound shirt that, if it had
seen better days, at least hadn't seen *too* many of them. No
rips, stains, or – and she wished she could say the same for the
cabin floor – muddy pawprints. It would have to do. She
paired the shirt with light capris and wound her hair into a
bun at the back of her head, and convinced herself she wasn't
entirely dispirited by the result.

"Any luck?" she asked, turning to Felix. He shook his
head. "Just going straight to voicemail still? Ugh, so much for
Pride Telco's one-hundred-percent coverage. I'll text them. At
least that might get through."

Lexi and Felix insisted on adding their own messages, but
eventually, all the lights in the cabin were turned off and the
kids settled down to sleep. Silence fell across the camping
ground.

Toni lay back on her bunk with a sigh of relief. Just as she
was closing her eyes, she heard something rustle in the bushes
outside. She held her breath, waiting for the noise to come
again, but there was nothing.

It must have been the wind, she told herself, and fell peace-
fully asleep.

FOUR
JACK

Jack wheeled the two mountain bikes to the start of the path where he had agreed to meet Toni. His own bike was a few years old, and had been hardly used during those years. He'd had to dig around in the garage to find it, hidden behind old boxes and building equipment. It had been so long since he'd been in the Silver Forest for any purpose, let alone to use the bike paths, that he'd wondered if it would still be in working condition. But, a few minutes with the tire pump and oil and it had been as good as new.

Well ... not quite. Because sitting right next to his bike was Toni's *actually* new bike. He had called into town and had it delivered first thing that morning, a top-of-the-line machine that gleamed in the sunlight. Next to it, 'good as new' looked more than a bit shabby.

Jack moved the bikes a bit further apart, but the difference between the two rigs was still clear. Toni's was obviously shop-new.

Too fast, he told himself. *She's going to realize you bought it especially for her. You're going to scare her off!*

He wondered if he should ding the bike up a bit before Toni got here—maybe kick some dust on it to get the shine off. Before he could do any of that, his tiger sat up and purred.

She's here!

"Toni," he greeted her, holding out his hand. She took it with a smile and he felt as though a bolt of lightning went straight from his hand to his groin. *Take her*, his tiger growled. *Make her yours!*

I'm already worried the bike is going to scare her off, he argued. *YOU'RE NOT HELPING.*

It wasn't only his tiger that had reacted to Toni's presence. He felt an indescribable urge just to touch her, to stay close to her; and the slight furrow between her eyebrows only made his protective instinct stronger.

It was bugging him, that instinct. De Jager hadn't made any further appearances, and no one had reported sighting him, so Jack figured he had just been passing through, not staying in the campground after all. And yet his tiger was still on the alert for danger.

It was probably because it had been so long since he shifted, Jack decided. He always got antsy if he had to spend long stretches of time in human form, and the last few months had been so busy with work he hadn't been able to spend any time in tiger form. This heightened awareness must be a result of his tiger being so eager to be let loose.

Soon, he told it reassuringly. *Maybe tonight. Unless...*

NOW, his tiger demanded. And that wasn't all. It insisted that the optimum course of action would be to literally gather Toni and the twins together and growl threateningly at anyone who came near ... but even if there was a real threat, that wasn't the sort of thing you could do as a human. And for Toni, he had to be a human.

Jack motioned toward the bikes. "There's this one place I really want you to see, but it's a bit far to walk. I hope you don't mind riding. I had to guess at the right size bike for you, but I think this one should be fine." *If it isn't, I'll get you another one,* he did *not* add.

Toni's eyes went wide, and Jack readied a handful of sentences, most of which began, *Oh this old thing? No, it's ... really old, yep ... what a coincidence it's the right size for you, eh?*

On second thought, he threw all of those sentences into his mental trash can.

"I'm..." Toni bit her lower lip. "I'm not a very confident cyclist. I mean, I learned when I was younger, but you'd have to be suicidal to cycle anywhere in my city..." She trailed off as Jack picked up a gleaming helmet – forget-me-not blue, it perfectly matched the bike's paint job – and brought it over to her.

"You'll be fine," he reassured her. "This is the smoothest, flattest path in the park. No jumps, no ravines, just following the river up to the perfect picnic spot." He saw her eyes flick to the pack he wore on his back. "Best of all, it's in the opposite direction to where Karen is taking the kids today. So you don't need to worry about bowling anyone over."

"Or being bowled over myself, more likely." Toni bit her bottom lip, still staring nervously at the bikes. Then she squared her shoulders and grinned at Jack. "Or falling off without any help from anyone, but what the hell. Let's go!"

Toni's smile sent a shock of heat through Jack's body. He

couldn't just *see* Toni's heady rush of excitement; he could feel it unfurling deep inside himself.

Was this another part of the mate bond? It was as though a tiny, precious part of his mate's soul was lodged inside him, glowing like a sun in his chest. He could feel they were distinctly *hers*, separate from his own feelings, but as he focused on them he felt the same excitement fill his own body.

With fingers made clumsy by joy, Jack fitted Toni's helmet on her head, adjusting the straps so that it fit closely over her tumbling curls.

This close, he could smell her skin under the masking smells of shampoo and deodorant, beneath the florals, a warm, musky scent that went straight to his head. And to other places. Jack stepped back and cleared his throat, hoping she wouldn't notice the sudden bulge in his trousers.

He held Toni's bike steady for her as she mounted it – she still hadn't said anything about how new it looked, so hopefully she hadn't even noticed – and then they were off, cruising slowly under the dappled shade of the trees.

The path was wide enough for the two of them to ride side-by-side. They rode along in silence, Jack not wanting to disturb Toni's concentration as she tested out the bike's gears and brakes. He was still glowing with the discovery of this new side of the mate bond, the deep connection he felt with her. Did she feel it, too?

He couldn't help glancing sideways at her. Toni was still getting used to the bike ... probably because her attention was clearly elsewhere. Jack's heart raced as he saw her shooting sideways glances back at him. More than once he caught Toni's eye as their glances intersected and left her blushing.

The path sloped gently down through the forest. The

human noise of the camping grounds faded away and was replaced by birdsong and the faint noise of moving water somewhere in the distance.

"Did Lexi and Felix get away okay this morning?" he asked as Toni started to relax on her bike.

"Oh, yes," Toni replied, wobbling a little. She steadied herself and continued, "I think all the racing around they did yesterday only left them with *more* energy today. I hope Karen and the coaches will be able to keep up with them." She sounded as though she had her doubts.

"Karen will be fine," Jack reassured her. "You know she punched a bear once?"

"No!"

"Well, a papier-mâché bear. It snuck up on her..."

Jack told the story with enough dramatic embellishments that Toni was soon giggling helplessly. He thrilled as her bubbling joy was reflected in his own heart – then felt a sickening swoop of vertigo.

Toni suddenly swerved and fell sideways, just sticking her foot out in time to stop herself falling over. She hopped along for a few feet, then regained her balance.

"Argh! Okay, no more funny stories." She laughed. "I think I can *just* handle the bike and talking at the same time, but laughing is a step too far."

A shadow passed over her face. Jack didn't need the mate bond to follow the path of her thoughts. Joking was out, so what would they talk about? Something more serious, and what was the first thing that would come to mind?

De Jager.

"Come on," he said softly. "We're almost at the picnic spot. I promise, no more jokes."

Toni swung herself back on to the bike and smiled. "Oh, I don't know ... It makes it more of a challenge, doesn't it? Like an obstacle course where the obstacles are my own inability to ride in a straight line."

They carried on down the path, but although she kept up a brave front, Jack could tell that even the thought of de Jager had shaken her. The glow in his heart was dulled, cautious. Afraid.

Jack's tiger growled in frustration. From its point of view, de Jager was worse than a competitor. He was an enemy who made Jack's mate feel unsafe. Jack could feel his tiger growing unhappier the longer Jack allowed the enemy to roam free in their territory.

There's nothing I can do about it, Jack insisted. *The man may be a waste of oxygen, but he hadn't done anything wrong. Even if he turns up again, the most I can do is throw him off my land.*

Even thinking the words left a bad taste in Jack's mouth. He hated that even the thought of de Jager could affect Toni so badly, and that there was nothing he could do about it.

You know what you should do! his tiger roared.

Jack's hands fumbled on the handlebars, and he looked down to see orange and black fur sprouting from his fingers, claws starting to flex. He hurriedly drew himself consciously back into his human body, focusing on human things: the feel of clothes on his body, his awareness of the careful engineering that went into making the bike ride so smooth, the prospect of unpacking the picnic later—

—Toni—

He shook his head and looked down again. His hands were, well, hands again. He flexed his fingers carefully over

the handlebars, adjusting his grip, and glanced guiltily sideways to see if Toni had noticed. She was glaring down at the
road in front of them, wobbling slightly, and didn't appear to
have noticed anything out of the ordinary. He gave a quiet sigh
of relief.

You're NOT helping, he growled silently to his tiger.

The last thing he wanted was for Toni to turn around and
think he'd been devoured by a mysteriously-appearing big cat.
Which – Jack knew his limits when it came to shifting – would
probably be wearing the ripped remains of his shorts and
t-shirt.

No. Toni had enough on her mind. Today would definitely benefit from a complete absence of mysteriously-
appearing, clothes-stealing giant tigers.

FIVE
TONI

Yes, it was a very smooth, gentle path.

Yes, her bike was perfectly sized for her, with the sort of suspension she wasn't used to even cars having, let alone bicycles.

Yes, she had discovered that if she just pointed herself in a direction and stared fixedly at, for example, a tree or particularly lovely patch of flowers in a straight line ahead of her, the bike would seemingly automatically head along that trajectory.

But...

Toni hadn't been exaggerating when she told Jack she wasn't a confident cyclist. She technically knew *how* to ride a bike, but it was taking most of her attention just to stay upright and headed in a straight line. Which was a problem, because her mind was constantly, ridiculously, gravitating unstoppably toward the incredibly handsome man riding next to her. Which meant, due to her follow-your-nose cycling style, she kept swooping sideways as though her bike was determined to mash up its wheels and chain with his.

For the eighth time (ninth? She was beginning to lose track) Toni snapped her eyes back on to the track in front of her and tried to steady herself before she careened into Jack.

Just as she had gotten steady again, he called out to her to stop. She pulled on the brakes, wobbled precariously back and forth for a few seconds, and then her weight overbalanced the bike and she began to tip over. She stuck out one foot to land on the dirt path —

—and found herself, for the second time in two days, in Jack Silver's arms.

"I've got you," he said, in the sort of voice that Toni knew would have caused a collision if she had still been on her bike. She hopped awkwardly on her one grounded foot and swung her other leg over the bike, which Jack grabbed and wheeled to the side of the track. He looked back at her and grinned.

"We're going to go a bit off-road here. There's a place I want you to see."

She rubbed her neck and followed Jack through the trees. Her bike might have had incredible suspension, but what the ride had lacked in bone-cracking jolts, her body had more than made up for in tight muscles.

There wasn't any path here, but Jack moved easily through the forest. Dappled sunlight lit his broad shoulders and bare arms as he held branches out of Toni's way, and she tried not to stare. The faint sound of rushing water became louder. Was there a river ahead? She imagined relaxing in the cool water, letting all the tension in her muscles wash away ... and maybe Jack would go for a swim, too...

Her attention wandering, Toni almost tripped over a tree root. Jack stopped and looked back at her.

"Are you okay?"

Toni blushed. *Only so distracted by the thought of you without that shirt on that I'm tripping over my own feet,* she thought, embarrassed. Out loud, she mumbled, "Um, yeah, no problem."

It was hard to judge distance in the forest, but Toni guessed they must have made their way at least a few hundred yards off-track before they arrived at a thick cluster of trees. Jack darted ahead of her, moving confidently across the uneven ground, and pulled aside a fall of mossy branches.

"Oh, that's ... it's beautiful," Toni gasped, taken unawares.

She had thought the forest was lovely, but the scene revealed behind the thicket of trees was like something from a calendar. The ferns and leaf-mold gave way to smooth gray stones as the ground sloped toward the river. She immediately saw the source of the sound of rushing water. A few yards upstream, the river cascaded down in a miniature waterfall, sending rainbow arcs of spray into the air. Below the waterfall, the river widened into a broad, still pool. Sunlight poured in through a gap in the trees and set everything glittering.

Toni walked forward, drunk on the sheer natural beauty of the hidden grotto.

She turned back, open-mouthed. Jack stood in front of the thicket, grinning proudly. She could see that the trees she had walked through hid this place completely from outside view, and they were far enough from the bike path that they couldn't hear any sign of other people. She could almost believe they were completely alone in the forest.

"It's just ... beautiful," she repeated, knowing the word didn't go nearly far enough to describe the place.

Jack ducked his head, although the proud grin still stretched across his face. "I found this spot before I bought Silver Forest. I think it's what finally convinced me to buy the land. The rest of the forest is great, but this..." He looked down again, as though he was embarrassed. "It's something special. I wanted to share it with you."

Toni's eyes widened. *Share it with her?*

She'd tried to tell herself that Jack was just being friendly by inviting her out today. She'd even wondered if he just felt sorry for her, being left on her own in the campground. But there was no pity in Jack's eyes as he glanced up at her.

No matter how much she tried to convince herself otherwise, the more she thought about it, this whole thing seemed more like ... a *date*.

Now there was a word so rusty it creaked. It wasn't that Toni had given up on romance in the past few years, but the few times she had met up with online-dating matches probably couldn't rightly be labelled 'dates'. 'Disasters', yes, but...

A soft breeze floated along the riverbank, ruffling Jack's hair. He was busily unpacking his backpack, and Toni let her gaze fall to his face. The strong, square jaw, softened by the gentle curve of his mouth. She wondered whether his lips were as soft as they looked.

"What do you think?" Jack asked.

Toni had been so focused on Jack himself that she hadn't noticed what he was unpacking. She had assumed they'd be eating sandwiches, but lined up on the riverbank were piles of expensive-looking boxes of food, utensils, and – a half-sized bottle of champagne?

Toni gulped.

This was *definitely* a date.

She walked slowly over to Jack, trying not to show how amazed she was – by the location, the food, *and* the ... date.

Unfortunately she was aware she was blushing far too much to make that believable.

"I didn't realize this was *that* sort of picnic," she said, pointing at the champagne. Jack's face fell. "I didn't – I mean – I'm not complaining. You know. If it is, um, that sort of picnic."

She blushed. More. In fact she was beginning to think that if Jack had packed marshmallows and crackers, he could have cooked s'mores on her cheeks.

Jack was looking down at the feast spread in front of him as though he had suddenly realized he had got things horribly wrong. "Toni, I'm sorry. I don't want to make you uncomfortable. This is too much, you're right, we should go back—"

Toni sat down in front of him. The smooth river stones shifted under her, making a comfortable hollow for her to settle into. She looked across at Jack, aware her face was still burning. "No, this is fine. It's more than fine. Really."

She was surprised by how true that was. She felt confident that Karen and the other competent adults she had left Lexi and Felix with would look after the kids. And she had, after all, been looking forward to a little innocent flirtation.

Though maybe the champagne meant the flirtation wasn't going to be *that* innocent...

She noticed, absently, that Jack's eyes had taken on the same golden cast she thought she had seen the day before when he was walking through the clearing. Did he always have a gold ring around his pupils, or was it only when the sun caught his eyes?

Toni realized she had been staring into Jack's eyes long enough that, now that she had noticed what she was doing, it became awkward. She looked away and her own eyes fell upon the unopened packages in front of Jack.

"What have we got here?" she asked, then cleared her throat. Her voice had gone all rough, and her mouth was suddenly dry. She licked her lips and glanced up to see Jack still watching her, his eyes glowing gold.

Jack stretched out his legs and leaned over, his previous moment of uncertainty dropping away. He looked across as her with a teasing smile, brown – golden-brown – eyes sparkling.

"I wasn't sure what you would like, so I ordered ... most of the menu, actually. Pastries, cold cuts, fruit ... and the champagne," he added. He smiled up at her as he poured her a glass, and all she could think about was the taste of his lips. She hadn't noticed before how enticingly the corners of his mouth curved up when he smiled.

"Here," he said, passing her a champagne flute, "to celebrate your first weekend at Silver Forest."

The words *the first of many* slunk into Toni's head. She pushed them away. *Where did that come from?*

To cover her distraction, she took a sip of champagne. The bubbles fizzed against her lips and she took another, slower sip, trying to gather her thoughts.

"This is wonderful, she said truthfully. "And everything smells delicious." Now that the packages were out of the chilled pack, tantalizing scents were beginning to fill the air.

"What would you like to try first?" Jack asked, grinning

happily. He picked up one of the containers and began to unwrap it.

"Wait," Toni said quickly, "I want to choose."

Jack laughed. "Without seeing what's in them?"

"Exactly." Toni licked her lips, which were still tingling. She ran her hands over the packages – stiff containers, little jars, mysterious items wrapped in sandwich paper and tape. Her eyes gleamed. "I pick something, and that's what we eat first. Maybe it's pastries, maybe it's dessert ... I want to be surprised."

"Then go ahead," Jack said, spreading his hands. "I leave our meal in your hands."

Toni examined the pile of hidden treats. She picked up a cardboard box and inhaled deeply. "Mmm ... I smell bready, crusty goodness..."

"The croissants?" Jack said hopefully.

Toni smiled slowly and set the box down.

"Be patient!"

She picked up a small, plastic container and felt its contents move as she lifted it. Small objects, not very heavy, shifted and settled as she held the package to her nose. Oh, yes.

"You know, this is the first picnic I've been on this summer," she said, pulling off the lid. "So I think we should start with ... summer berries."

She revealed a basket of bright, juicy berries. Strawberries, raspberries, blueberries, and...

"What are these?" she wondered, plucking out one of the bright orange, raspberry-like berries.

"Those are cloudberries," Jack explained. "So called because of their resemblance to, er, clouds."

"Ah, yes," Toni murmured. "Clouds are famously yellow, of course." She popped the berry into her mouth. "Oh, that's tart!"

"Here," Jack said, putting his hand into the basket. "Something sweet to cut the taste." He held out a bright red strawberry.

Toni started to reach for it, then paused. She didn't like to assume, but he was holding the berry up a bit higher than was necessary for him to pass it to her. A bit closer to her mouth, in fact.

She leaned forward. The scent of the strawberry filled her nose, the sweet, fresh smell she had always associated with summer. And these berries looked so much better than any she ever saw in the stores back home. She opened her mouth.

The strawberry was delicious. It was, as she had expected, the best strawberry she had ever eaten. It definitely cut through the tartness of the cloudberry, just as Jack had said.

She barely noticed it.

Her lips closed around the red berry and just brushed against the tips of Jack's fingers. Skin met warm skin and a jolt of heat burst from Toni's lips directly to between her legs. She moaned – quietly, she had thought, but evidently not quietly enough. She met Jack's eyes and knew he had heard her.

"Another?" he asked softly, his voice husky with desire. Toni's whole body ached at the sound of his voice, his clear longing. It was as though that one touch had set off a fire inside her, and only the feel of his hands on her could quench it.

Or inflame it more.

"Yes," she whispered. She blindly plucked another berry from the basket and, hand trembling, lifted it to his lips.

Jack kissed her fingers, and caught the blueberry between

his teeth. Toni leaned toward him as he looked up, eyes burning gold under heavy lids. He pressed his lips against hers, crushing the berry between them. Juice burst against Toni's teeth as she pushed hungrily into him, deepening the kiss.

Jack moved over her, cradling her head in one hand. Toni gasped as his other hand slid up the side of her body, his touch tantalizingly gentle.

Something cold landed on her shoulder. She broke the kiss and looked down, disconcerted. A plump, pink raspberry was nestled on her collarbone.

"Hmm," Jack murmured. "Where did that come from?" He trailed kisses down her neck and kissed off the berry, carefully licking away all traces of juice. "Mmm. That's better."

Toni lay back on the smooth river stones, feeling them shift under her. Jack moved with her, covering her body with his. He was hot against her, the heat of his body burning through their clothes. He lowered himself further to nuzzle her collarbone and she felt the hard shaft of his erection press again her leg.

"O-oh," Toni gasped. "I think … you'd better make sure there aren't any more."

She felt Jack smile against her skin, and then his hands were at the knot that tied her wraparound shirt in place. He took his time untying it, until Toni could have screamed with frustration. Then she felt the cool breeze running over her tops of her breasts as he pulled the fabric aside.

"Toni … God, you're so gorgeous," he whispered, as though he was under a spell he didn't want to break. "I'm the luckiest man in the world."

Toni squirmed under his gaze and he put one hand on her

cheek, turning her head so she was looking straight into his eyes. "I'm not lying, Toni. You are the most exquisite woman I have ever seen. Your eyes, your lips – God, your breasts..." His hands ran over her, setting her skin on fire with lust. "I could just look at you forever."

"*Don't*," she gasped, the berry game forgotten. "Don't just look. I want you. Jack, I've never wanted anyone as much as I want you right now..."

He smiled slyly up at her, resting one cheek against her breast. Toni was wet already, wet and ready, desperately ready. A small part of her brain was surprised at herself – shocked even – but she ignored it. She had spent the last few years miserably failing to make any sort of connection with any man. Why shouldn't she enjoy herself now she had the chance, even if it was just for the weekend?

Then he unhooked her bra and buried his face between her breasts, and all her thoughts flew away.

Jack caressed her breast, kissing his way up to her nipple and then teasing it with long, slow licks. She felt her tender skin stiffen and peak under his tongue and a jolt of arousal sparked between her legs. Shamelessly, she pressed herself against him, finding the hard bulge in his trousers and rubbing herself against it. "I need you," she moaned, and was rewarded with an inarticulate groan that reverberated against her skin.

He fumbled with her fly and she raised herself against him just as he loosened her pants to pull them down over her ass, and his hand pressed between her legs. She almost came just from the feel of him touching her. Her whole body quivered as he gently pressed his fingers into her folds. He brushed against the nub of her clit and she gasped, quivering against him.

"May I?" he murmured, looking up at her through those

dark lashes. His pupils were huge with lust, the irises no more than a thin gold band. Toni almost cried out with frustration.

"Yes – please!" she gasped.

He lowered himself against her, his lips brushing against her round stomach, her hips, the delicate skin at the tops of her legs. Then he buried his face between her legs, his tongue darting out to taste her, to explore every inch of her most intimate place. She moaned as he found her clit again and teased it, circling it with his tongue. One of his hands slid under her ass and squeezed. Her body thrilled at his touch – at his touching her everywhere. But it wasn't enough. She strained against him. "Please – I need you inside me."

He moaned something against her and she felt his fingers probe the slick flesh of her pussy. God, she was so wet. Her body was thrumming with desire, she just needed – she needed—

Jack dipped one finger inside her, then another, moving them slowly in and out. Her body reacted instinctively, tightening around him so that she could feel every inch he pressed inside her. His fingers brushed a sensitive spot inside her and she flexed into the touch. *Yes*, she thought desperately. *There, there – <there!>*

Toni cried out as her orgasm built and broke inside her, sending shockwaves of pleasure through her body. Her pussy clenched against Jack's soaking fingers as he rubbed against her g-spot, drawing every last whimper and shudder out of her orgasm.

"Oh, my God," she murmured as she relaxed back on to the stony bank. "Jack, that was ... that was..."

Words failed her. She stopped trying to describe it and simply flung her arms wide, sighing in satisfaction.

Jack traced a pattern on her thigh. Her skin still thrilled under his touch. Even though she had just had the most immense orgasm of her life, she felt her body respond to him.

"Do you want..." she started, still tongue-tied from exhausted satisfaction. Jack sat up and looked down at her with a look of distinct smugness on his face.

"Do I want ... lunch?" he asked innocently.

Toni groaned and mock-slapped his arm. He grabbed his hand and planted a kiss on it.

"No – I think I want a swim," he decided, eyes dancing wickedly.

In one fluid motion he stood up and stripped off his shirt, revealing a tanned, muscled chest and the tempting hint of a treasure-trail leading under his pants. He winked at her, turned around and unfastened his belt. His back was broad, with long, lean muscles moving smoothly under his skin. He pulled off his pants and stood naked in front of Toni, looking back at her over his shoulder.

"Feel free to join me," he murmured over his shoulder, and slid effortlessly into the water.

Toni raised herself up on her elbows and enjoyed the sight of Jack ducking under the water and surfacing, every inch of him glistening in the sunlight. He was without a doubt the most handsome man she had ever seen. If she didn't have the evidence of her missing shirt and swooning body to hand, she wouldn't have believed he would ever be interested in a girl like her.

But interested he was. More than interested. Toni had never had any man treat her like this. Jack looked at her like she was a goddess; she was used to men ignoring her curves, or putting up with them, but Jack had embraced every plump inch of her body as though he couldn't get enough of her.

And she couldn't get enough of him. Her orgasm hadn't left her sated – just the opposite. She was bursting with energy, on fire with longing. She wanted more. She wanted more, *now*.

Toni stood up, leaving her shirt on the ground. Her shorts and panties were already around her ankles; she stepped out of them. Jack was watching her from the pool, eyes dark with lust. She took a few unsteady steps toward the river, Jack's eyes tracking her every movement.

She put one foot in the water. "Oh – it's cold!"

"It's warmer over here," Jack replied. She looked over at him. The water was very clear – and even taking into account the fact that things under water looked a bit different due to the way the water bent the light, she could tell that he wasn't having *any* issues with the cold. His cock was thick and long, and ready for her. Just like she was ready for him. She took another step and shivered with anticipation.

Jack swam up to her. The river bed was shallow where she was standing, but quickly fell away, so that while she was only ankle-deep he, only a few feet away, was treading water. "Come on in," he said invitingly. "I promise I'll make it worth your while."

"You already made it *worth my while* on the shore," Toni countered. Goosebumps were making their way up her legs. Despite the warm weather, the river was almost icy.

"Hmm," Jack hummed non-commitally. "I think I have something more to offer."

God, she wanted him so badly. Her desire was like a drum inside her, so loud she could barely hear.

But the water was *so cold*.

Toni stared at the gorgeous man in front of her. She imagined his toned body under hers, his strong hands claiming her body for his own, his hard cock thrusting into her slick centre.

Cold water be damned.

She closed her eyes, held her breath, and dived in. Icy water closed over her head like a knife. Her skin tingled with the shock. Then warm hands were pulling her upwards, pulling her legs to wrap around his waist. Her head broke the surface and she laughed.

"Oh – I think – I think you're going to have to help warm me up," she gasped, catching her breath. Her hands slid over Jack's broad shoulders and down his back as she leaned in to him. The water was cold, yes, bitterly cold – but he was hot under her. She pressed herself against him, luxuriating in the feeling of his skin against hers, his body heating her body.

They were so close that Toni could see every bead of water that clung to Jack's face, making him look as though his brow and lashes were dripping with diamonds. He lay back in the water so that Toni was on top of him, and she worried briefly before realizing he was keeping them both afloat with slow kicks of his long, powerful legs. She ran her arms down his back, feeling the muscles shift under his skin.

"You're not going to get distracted and dunk us?" she murmured, trailing kisses along his jaw.

She felt, rather than heard, him moan in response.

Seconds later she felt water rush over her as he twisted sideways. They drifted together in the water until she felt smooth riverstones against her back.

The bank of the swimming hole was so steep that even with her torso and hips resting on the rocks, her legs were still floating free in the water. She stroked Jack's legs with her own, drawing him closer.

Jack swam up to the bank and slowly raised himself up on top of Toni. She looked into his eyes and even though she was settled on the riverbank it was like she was drowning in those two golden pools. Her own eyes were half-shut, lids heavy with a desire that thrummed through her whole body. She felt her heart hammering in her chest, so hard she thought she might fly apart. "Please," she whispered, "I need you inside me."

Jack leant down and kissed her, long and gentle. His tongue brushed over her lips, teasing them open, and she surrendered, letting him enjoy her.

She felt a touch between her thighs and parted her legs, wrapping them around Jack's waist. The tip of his cock brushed against her entrance, teasingly slow. "Are you ready?" Jack murmured into her mouth.

"Yes!"

She was slick, and willing, and his cock slid inside her like it was meant to be there. Toni moaned and arched her back as he pushed his full length inside her at once, filling her completely. She had never been with someone this big before, and the feeling was almost overwhelming. He pinned her to the bank, pumping in and out of her with exquisite slowness. Lost in sensation, Toni closed her eyes, letting the waves of pleasure build up inside her, higher, higher, until she couldn't hold them back any more.

Toni's first orgasm had burst out of her like a flooding dam, but this one was like a tidal wave. It grew inside her, wave after wave, filling her with pleasure. When she finally came it was with a sensation of being utterly grounded, not of falling apart but of finding herself, safely gathered in this man's arms. She clung to Jack and kissed him deeply, trying to hold on to the sensation for as long as possible as her body shuddered and clenched.

"Oh god – Toni—" Jack gasped, and she felt his cock twitch inside her as he came. He bore down on her, cradling her head in one hand and clutching her waist with the other. Finally they lay still together, cool water lapping over their heated bodies.

"Oh, my darling," Jack said, his voice muffled by Toni's hair. "I wish we could stay here forever."

Toni shifted. He was still inside her, and even the thought of that sent a thrill of excitement down her spine. "Mmm," she agreed, rolling her hips against his.

In the end they didn't stay there forever; but it was quite some time before they moved again.

SIX
JACK

JACK WAS HAPPIER THAN HE HAD EVER BEEN IN HIS LIFE. He was almost purring – in fact, he wasn't sure that he *wasn't* purring. He wanted to stretch and yawn, extend his claws and settle down in the sun in ear-twitching, tail-flicking pleasure.

No, he thought firmly. *Human. Human pleasure.*

He decided he could still lie down and stretch, but no sooner had he done that than he jumped to his feet again. Toni, who had been lying beside him, eyes shut as she basked in the sun, raised herself up on her elbows and looked at him quizzically.

"You must be starving," he exclaimed, just as his stomach growled and gave away the more selfish side of his plan.

Toni laughed and lay back down. He quickly gathered together an armful of the scattered containers of food, and the small bottle of champagne.

He held out a flaky *pain au chocolat* under Toni's nose and she inhaled happily. "Mmm – yes, please," she said, opening her mouth wide. He paused for a moment – only slightly distracted by the sight of her plump red lips parted for him – and placed the corner of the pastry between them. Toni chewed and sighed appreciatively. "Oh, that is delicious."

"Can I interest you in another? And a pillow, perhaps?" Jack offered, lying down behind her head. She grinned and shuffled backwards so her head was resting on his chest. He fed her the rest of the chocolatey treat, taking care to ensure lots of crumbs fell on her neck and breast for him to clean away. His hand lingered on her breast, feeling its soft weight, the gentle movement as she breathed.

"Jack," Toni murmured, her voice muzzy with sleep and happiness. "Jack, this is possibly the best day I have ever had."

"I was about to say the same thing," he replied, looking down at her. She looked the very picture of contented peace: eyes closed, breathing slow, a gentle smile curving her lips. He was just wondering whether to give in to the impulse to swoop in and plant a kiss on those lips when Toni's eyes shot open, sparkling with playfulness. She rolled over, resting her forearms on either side of Jack's broad chest and smiling down at him.

"So," she said, a teasing glint in her eye, "I'm pretty sure someone promised me a terrible, embarrassing story about being Jack Silver of Silver Forest, house, and ... did you say there was a mine, as well?"

Jack groaned theatrically and let his head fall back with a thump. "Yes. And ... it's a silver mine."

Toni chortled disbelievingly. "Oh, you have got to be joking. That is just too much to believe."

Jack spread his arms wide. "What can I say? I'm very

suggestible." He was about to make another joke, but stopped. He could laugh about it all day, entertain Toni with anecdotes and stories, but why not tell her the truth?

After all, he thought, guilt twisting in his stomach, he was going to be telling her enough lies in this relationship.

"Actually," he began, and had to stop to clear his throat. "Actually, the whole Silver thing isn't a coincidence. My family used to live here – generations of us, until the mine failed when my father was a kid and they had to sell up to keep bread on the table. As soon as I had the money, buying this place back was the first thing I did."

"So this isn't the conservation trust's land, it's yours. Your dad must have been so proud, to see you get the family land back," Toni said warmly.

Jack had to look away from her.

"My parents died when I was in high school."

"Oh, Jack, I'm so sorry," Toni gasped, her voice full of concern. She reached out one hand and cradled his cheek. "That was thoughtless of me, I shouldn't have…"

"You couldn't have known," Jack interrupted, putting his arms around her. She was so warm, and soft, the perfect weight against his body. He sighed. If his parents hadn't died when he was still so young, might they have been able to help him figure out how to deal with his mate being human, not a shifter? His parents had told him a little about shifter abilities, and the mate bond – a child-friendly version of it at least.

But not enough. Jack could only imagine that his parents had meant to tell him more once he was older, but that had never happened. His mother and father had been killed in a car crash when he was fourteen. Jack had been sent to live with his mother's family, who didn't want to hear anything about shifters, despite the fact that his mother had been one.

As an adult, he'd met many other shifters, but had been embarrassed to ask questions about knowledge they seemed to take for granted. How a non-shifting family could produce a shifter like his mother. How his tiger was a part of him, but it sometimes felt stronger, more powerful, and other times was quiet.

How the mate bond worked.

How having a mate bond with a *human* worked. If it could work at all.

"I didn't mean to bring back any bad memories," Toni was saying, concern in her voice. Jack held her tightly and kissed the top of her head. He could feel her heartbeat against his chest, and her concern for him wasn't only evident in her voice. He felt her love in that warm glow in his own chest, growing to enfold Jack like an embrace.

Maybe he would never know more about being a shifter. Maybe he would have to hide that side of himself, ignore it, put it away. But if things worked out today, he would have Toni. And that would be worth it.

Wouldn't it?

He kissed her again. "It was a long time ago. And not really the sort of thing I'd usually bring up on a first, um."

She raised her eyebrows. "A first *um*? Is that what this is?"

Jack knew Toni was deliberately steering the conversation back to lighter topics, and he was thankful for it. "Er ... picnic? Is that the word I'm looking for?"

Toni rolled her eyes and flopped back down on Jack's chest.

"Today has been ... I mean, I normally wouldn't do anything like this, but it's been wonderful," she mumbled into his chest. "Thank you. Seriously, at this point you could probably straight-up tell me that you secretly arranged the whole de Jager creepiness just to get me on this *um picnic*, and I'd be happy. Even without him freaking me out yesterday, the last few months have been ... well, not great. It's nice to have a break."

Jack stroked her back, and felt her sigh again.

"Really? You'd forgive me for tricking you?" he asked. But even as he said it, he knew he was venturing onto thin ice.

"Well ... no, that was more what some people call 'exaggeration for comic effect,'" Toni teased. "You lying to me would make all the *um* a bit awkward, wouldn't it?"

"Right," Jack replied, trying to smile back at her. Inside, he was cursing himself. He knew that any relationship he had with Toni would mean lying to her about his true nature, so why punish himself further by proving how cruel a betrayal that would be?

Lost in his own guilty thoughts, Jack barely noticed Toni roll over. She lay with her head and shoulder on his chest, staring up at the clear blue sky.

"I just..." she began softly, and Jack felt the sharp pang of self-doubt come through his connection to her. "I wish I knew *what* it was about him that got me so freaked out. I've been thinking about it, and he didn't actually do anything that ... bad?"

"I saw how much he scared you," Jack said simply. "That's bad enough for me."

"And if you hadn't been there? How would it have

sounded if I'd only told you about it afterward? Oh, there was this guy, and he terrified me more than anyone else has in my life, because he ... what, came up and introduced himself? Stood a little too close, like every garden-variety letch?" She threw up her hands. "And just to add the cherry on top of the crazy cake, I could then tell you about how his tablet – thing – *bit* me, only, oh, yeah, there's no proof of that anymore either." Toni flexed her unblemished fingers in the sunlight.

"Well, I was there. I saw what he was like. And if saying his tablet bit you is crazy, then I'm crazy too. I saw your fingers after you picked it up. It looked as though you'd tried to pick up a red-hot poker." Jack caught Toni's hand and drew it to his lips, gently kissing her fingertips. "I guess you're a fast healer."

"Hmm. Maybe. What a way to find it out, though."

"You didn't know?"

Toni shrugged, her shoulders rolling enjoyably over the planes of Jack's chest. "My – my folks have always been, well, fast healers. My plan has always been to just never get injured in the first place." Her voice was growing drowsy. "I guess ... I guess I was scared. I didn't want to find out that I *couldn't* heal as fast as Ellie, or Mom and Dad. Didn't want it to be something else that made me different..."

Her voice trailed off.

Jack's heart was racing. Fast healing? He might not know much about shifters, but he knew that fast healing was something all shifters shared. Even before he'd first shifted into his tiger form, he'd healed quickly, scrapes and bruises disappearing within a day, if not hours. So if Toni – if her family—

"Toni," he said quietly, then stopped, tongue-tied. How could he even start to phrase the question?

Then he realized the choice had been taken out of his

hands. Toni's eyes were closed, her chest rising and falling. She had fallen asleep.

Jack shook his head. This was probably for the best. His mind was connecting dots that weren't there.

With a sigh, he closed his eyes and fell asleep, cradling her in his arms.

SEVEN
TONI

Toni couldn't keep the smile off her face. She had woken from an incredible dream – and into an even better one. She and Jack spent the afternoon in lazy, intimate happiness, sharing the picnic and the champagne, and slipping in and out of the pool with its shimmering waterfall.

Not to mention all the ... exercise. They had made love again and again, slowly, as though they had all the time in the world. But with the sun falling over the treetops, both of them had realized it was time to leave. Jack had 'helped' Toni back into her clothes, kissing every inch of her skin before he covered it up.

Even now, Toni felt as though she was floating a foot above the path rather than pacing along it. Golden shafts of light pierced the green canopy above them, lending a warm glow to the path and the ferns and flowers at its sides. The whole forest seemed to be under a spell of beauty and calmness.

Even now, even just walking together along the gravel path, Toni could barely keep her hands off Jack. They were walking with a little space between them, a teasing gap that just begged to be crossed. Toni reached out and, without looking, her questing fingers met Jack's. He lifted her hand and nuzzled the underside of her wrist.

They had just reached the end of the track when she heard it. Not a word, nothing said aloud – only a scream that echoed through her mind, and was suddenly cut off.

Toni's breath caught in her throat. <*Lexi! Felix!*> she called, only just remembering to use mindspeak and not scream their names aloud. Beside her, Jack froze, his grip on her wrist tightening.

"I—" Toni stammered, words failing her. Neither of the children responded to her silent cry, though she was positive it was their scream she had heard. She felt herself go pale, skin prickly and cold. She pulled her hand out of Jack's grasp and dropped the bike. "I've – I've got to go."

Toni broke into a run. She barely knew what direction she was running in, but her legs pushed on, leaves and gravel crunching under her feet. She burst through the trees into open ground and just had time to recognise the clearing with the bike ramps and jumps before she collided with Karen.

The blonde woman's face was wracked with worry. "Toni, I—"

"Where are they?" Toni gasped. Inside she was still calling out, <*Kids, where are you? Just shout out, let me know you're okay!*>

Karen's eyes flickered from Toni's to a point behind her and she felt, rather than heard, Jack run up to stand at her shoulder.

Karen ran a hand through her hair and grimaced. "Toni,

there you are. I don't want to worry you, but I'm not sure where Felix and Lexi have gotten to..."

Jack put one hand on Toni's shoulder and she shrugged it off, mind racing. God, she was so stupid. How had she ever thought she could spend a day apart from the kids and they would stay safe? She should have known that no human babysitters would be a match for the two shifter children. And now—

She called out to the twins again, desperately hoping to hear an answer, any answer.

Nothing.

Something had happened to them. She didn't want to think what. She couldn't.

"I have to go," she stammered. "I have to – have to call—"

"Toni, calm down. Listen to me." Jack had both hands on her shoulders and was looking down into her eyes.

Toni realized she was hyperventilating, her pulse racing. She tried to control her breathing.

If Lexi and Felix couldn't even mindspeak to her...

Toni felt herself crumble as the evidence lined up in front of her. If Lexi and Felix were ever in real danger, no matter what the risk of revealing their shifter identities, they would transform. There were few places they couldn't escape from in cat form. And, human or cat, they would still be able to call out to her.

Unless someone already knew they might shift, and took precautions to prevent their escape that way.

Toni clenched her fists until her fingers stung. Stung like they'd been burnt.

De Jager. And that *thing*, whatever it was, that he'd been

so intent on when she first saw him. He had to have something to do with this.

With growing horror, Toni looked back on the events of the previous evening in a new light. De Jager must have been in the campground the whole time. But he'd only approached her after he'd seen her with the twins.

After Felix had been mindspeaking with her.

Could the device de Jager had been using – Toni's mind reeled – some sort of tracker that picked up on mindspeak? And – he must have deliberately dropped it in front of her. The way it had stung her ... it had looked like a burn, but it had *felt* as though it had scraped skin off her fingertips where she touched it.

Skin. Blood. DNA.

Toni gulped.

Of course. He wouldn't have been able to go up to the kids, but an adult, a related adult, was fair game. Toni's shifter genes weren't active, but they were still *there*. All those doctors' visits when she was young had proved that.

After picking up on Felix's mindspeak, and her defective DNA, de Jager would have had enough evidence to figure out who the shifters were in their little trio.

And if he had the technology to do all that ... Jack had said de Jager was a hunter. He wouldn't want to leave shifters any advantage. If he could detect mindspeak, it made sense that he would also have the ability to silence it.

It made sense. But it didn't. It made no sense. The most important rule of shifter society, no matter whether you were a cat or a four-toed sloth, was secrecy. How could a human know enough about them to be able to build that sort of technology?

Assuming de Jager was human.

The possibilities raised by that thought were too horrifying. Either de Jager was a shifter who hunted his own kind – knowing they couldn't appeal to human authorities for help – or he'd somehow had access to shifter abilities, enough to test and prove his hunting tech. Toni didn't want to think about what that might have involved.

She pushed it to the back of her mind. *Focus on what's happening now*, she told herself. *Find Lexi. Find Felix.*

She looked up at Jack, at the concern in his eyes. She trusted him, more deeply that she would ever have felt was possible given they had only known each other less than twenty-four hours. She had to tell him.

She couldn't.

Even if some humans already knew about shifters, telling more would only increase the danger. Even if she trusted the human in question. Even if she...

Jack was still talking to her, words that didn't make it to her ears. She made up her mind and held up one hand to his lips.

"De Jager has Lexi and Felix," she said quickly.

Karen gasped. "How can you know—"

"I can't explain that to you now. But he's got them, and they're still somewhere near the camp site. We have to move quickly." Toni had been speaking directly to Jack, but now she turned to look at Karen. "Have there been ... has anyone seen two small cats around the camp? Short-haired, with chocolate-brown fur. They're..." She thought quickly "...the twins' pets. He might have used them to, to blackmail them into going with him."

Karen frowned. "I haven't heard anything. Though I did

see an animal control van near the reception hut when we came back from today's ride."

Toni was running before she finished speaking. The reception building was at the entrance to the camping ground – down the road, past the cabins. She heard Karen shout in confusion behind her, but ignored it.

Jack ran up beside her, keeping pace with Toni's panicked sprint.

"This way. It's a shortcut," he said, pointing to another path through the trees.

Toni swerved to follow him, trying to keep her mental map of the park oriented. This route would bypass the cabins. If it went directly to the park entrance, it could save them minutes of running. And she had the feeling that every minute was going to count.

It was getting dark. They had been gone all day – *and that was the plan,* Toni wailed to herself, *leave the kids to their own devices– with an adult who had no idea they were shifters. How did I ever, ever think that would be a good idea?*

Toni had a stitch in her side by the time they burst out of the trees and on to sealed road. Ahead, the reception hut glowed like a beacon. The porch light illuminated a dark van parked in front.

Three hundred feet. Less. Toni opened her mouth to yell as the hut door opened and a man stepped out, two carry-cages clutched one in each hand. As she drew breath to shout, a panicked howl shot through her mind.

<HEEEELP!>

The cry cut into Toni like a knife. She stumbled and crashed to the ground. Beside her, Jack swore and clutched his head.

Toni tried to push herself back upright and hissed in pain as her wrist collapsed under her. She had hit the tarmac at running speed and tumbled head-over-heels; she didn't need the fading evening light to know the concrete had torn up the skin on her hands and knees. The side of her face stung.

"Are you all right?" Jack's voice was urgent, panting after their run. He knelt and pulled Toni upright.

Toni leant against him for support, testing her legs. It hurt, but she could stand the pain – and she could *stand*. Only her right wrist was really injured. She flexed her fingers gingerly, wincing as pain shot up her arm. Then she heard something that made her skin go cold.

Ahead of them – still too far ahead – the engine of the black van rumbled into life. Two headlights cut through the darkness, blinding Toni with their glare. She held one hand up to shield her eyes and shouted.

"Hey! Stop! You, stop right now!"

It was impossible to see the man behind the wheel. As Toni shouted and waved, Jack doing the same beside her, the headlights slipped sideways, leaving them in darkness. The engine roared, and the van swung away into the night.

Toni couldn't believe what she was seeing. She stood stunned for a moment, her head thumping.

He's driving away.

He saw two people yelling at him to stop, one of them bleeding on the road. And he drove away.

She realized with a chill of horror what that meant. It couldn't be an accident that the driver had sped off without checking to see whether she was okay.

It must have been de Jager. He hadn't stopped, because he recognised her – and he had Lexi and Felix.

And he knew who they were, too. *What* they were.

"No!" she cried, and ran forward again. It was no use. The van was far ahead of them already, and accelerating. But she couldn't stop. She couldn't just leave them.

"Toni, wait!" called Jack from behind her. He caught up to her in a few long strides and flung his arms around her, holding her still. Sobs heaved out of Toni and she pushed him away.

"I can't stop! I've got to – I've got to do something. He's got them—"

She stopped. How was she meant to explain this? He and Karen and everyone else would help her look for Lexi and Felix, but they were looking for human children. If she told Jack they had to go after the animal control van instead, he was going to think she had gone nuts. If she told him the twins were in the van – that they had just seen someone carrying them into the trunk in cages...

They'd lock her up. They would give her something to calm her down and keep her out of the way and keep looking around the camp for freaking *human* children and she would never be able to find Lexi and Felix. She would lose them.

No. She had to do this herself. But first...

Toni pressed the palms of her hands against her eyes, groaning. She had to call her sister, Ellie, and her husband. She only hoped they would answer this time. If she couldn't get hold of Ellie or Werther, then she would try her parents. Maybe they knew some local shifters through their own networks. Maybe they knew someone who could help.

She turned toward the reception hut, remembering the old rotary-style phone on the front desk.

"I'm sorry. I've got to – I've got to make a phone call..."

"Toni," Jack said again, grabbing her arm to stop her. Fury bubbled up inside her – how dare he stop her? Didn't he understand? But then she looked up into his eyes.

There was no pity or look of *oh-god-she's-lost-it-now* in his expression. Just care, concern, and ... something else.

"Toni," he repeated. "Lexi and Felix ... are in the truck, aren't they? When the guy with the cages came out, I heard..."

He looked at her as though a light had gone on behind his eyes.

"Toni, you trust me, don't you?"

"Yes," she blurted. "I do, but—"

He cut her off. "Then trust me now. I'll get the twins back. The road here has speed bumps all the way back to the highway. That van won't get far fast." He cupped Toni's face in his hands. "I will get them back."

Toni's eyes went wide. If he was going to go after the van, after the cats – was he suggesting – did that mean—? She didn't dare complete the thought. Before she could speak, he turned and ran into the darkness by the side of the road.

"Jack!" Toni strained to look into the shadows. She heard twigs breaking and footfalls muffled by leaf mold, and then nothing.

Toni shivered, adrenaline fading into fear and exhaustion. Whatever thought had half-formed as Jack reassured her was dissolving now.

What was he thinking? No human could keep pace with a speeding van, regardless of speed bumps. And he was joking if he thought he was going to catch up with the vehicle. It must be a mile away by now.

She was on her own.

First things first. Toni forced herself to jog over to the

reception hut. It was empty. There were no other cars around, either. She dredged Ellie's cell number out of her memory and picked up the phone.

There was no dial tone. She realized, dully, that this did not surprise her. Reception empty, a fake animal control van – of course they would cut the phone lines as well. Literally *cut* in this case, she saw as she followed the phone line back toward the wall.

Her cell was still in her pack in the cabin. She had left it there this morning because reception out here was so patchy the phone was useless, but she could drive back toward civilisation until she found a signal.

Maybe she would even catch up with the van on the way.

EIGHT
JACK

JACK RAN THROUGH THE UNDERGROWTH, A SILENT shadow in the night. The road out of the park wound through the outskirts of the forest, but in this form he could take a direct route through the trees. He could hear the roar of the van's engine ahead, crawling around the winding road.

It had been too long since he last shifted. This trip back to America was meant to be a holiday for his tiger, too, but what with one thing and another he hadn't had the chance to let it out.

Muscles bunched and stretched under striped fur as Jack leapt past shrubs and low-hanging branches. His strong night-vision meant he avoided the obstacles that would have tripped his human form, and he closed in on his prey.

While his tiger focused on the hunt, Jack's human mind was spilling over with questions. He knew that Toni was human – or he had assumed she was. Surely his tiger would have recognised a fellow shifter?

But her niece and nephew? Toni had panicked when

Karen told her two cats had been picked up by animal control. She had said they were the kids' pets, but ... why had she never mentioned them before? And who brought pet cats on a camping holiday?

As soon as she had heard about the two cats, she had run. The fear Jack smelled rolling off her was the same protective terror she'd had when Karen first told her the kids were missing.

The pieces started to fall into place. Why Toni had been so worried Karen wouldn't be able to keep the kids under control. The piercing screams from the van that had made her trip over. She hadn't fallen from surprise, she'd been reacting to the mental punch of the kids' terror flooding into her mind. He had felt it, too, but had thought the shooting pain was a result of the mate bond, and that he had been feeling Toni hurting as she hit the ground.

Toni knew about shifters. Hell, she might even be a shifter! He hadn't sensed it in her – but then he hadn't sensed that the twins were shifters, either.

The realisation fuelled him with elation and he ran faster. He could tell her about himself, talk to her about the mate bond. She would already know about it, if she came from a family of shifters. She would understand. She could probably tell him things about being a shifter that he didn't know.

He could tell her, and it wouldn't scare her off.

Yellow light glinted on distant trees, and Jack bared his fangs.

She would understand, but only if he could fix this, and save her niece and nephew. Otherwise he would just be the coward who had spent so long worrying about his *own* secret that he didn't see what was right under his nose. The great big tough tiger who was so self-involved he didn't even notice two tiny, helpless housecats.

Who let hunters take cubs from *his* land. From *his* mate.

His family.

He growled low in his throat. *That isn't going to happen*, he promised.

Jack knew the Silver Forest like the back of his paw. Just in front of him was the only section of road that cut through the rolling foothills rather than curling around them. Low cliffs lined the road on either side for a quarter-mile where dyna-mite had blown a flat track through the rock. Rather than following the flat ground, Jack loped up the side of the hill, watching the twin beams of the van's headlights dogleg along the winding road and begin to approach the cut. Crouching on the cliff above the road, he waited, every muscle tensed for action.

He had to time this right. He would only have one chance. One chance to save the children, and win Toni's trust.

The sound of the car engines grew louder. The driver was fighting a losing battle with the many speed-bumps that pock-marked the road. Jack had had them installed when he purchased the park, to reduce the danger of traffic accidents from drivers racing along the quiet road at high speeds. That decision was now proving a good one.

Jack watched as the van bumped over another obstacle and landed with a suspension-mauling screech.

Thirty feet. Twenty. Ten—

Jack leapt, landing with a squeal of claws on metal on the van's hood. A pale face stared at him in shock from the driver's seat. He just had time to note the driver wasn't de Jager before the man hit the brakes and sent the van spinning toward the side of the road.

Jack jumped aside as the vehicle ploughed through the barrier and into the cliff. Without waiting to see what happened to the driver he ran up to the doors at the back of the van. There was no need to shift to open them – human fingers might be able to work the locking mechanism but a tiger's claws could simply tear it off. The doors rattled open and Jack lifted his front legs on to the van floor to look inside.

Two heavy-duty wire carry-cages, the sort rangers used to trap feral animals in, were strapped to the back wall. Inside each was a small, chocolate-brown cat. They both froze in place, staring at him with wide blue eyes. The one on the left hissed at him, then backed to the far corner of its cage.

<Lexi – Felix – don't be afraid> he said, hoping his tone would have more sway with them than his giant teeth. *<Toni sent me, I ... you can't hear me, can you?>*

He paused, listening. The two cats *smelled* like shifters, but he couldn't hear a peep of mindspeak from either of them. He had heard them scream earlier, so he knew they could talk.

No, he remembered. *I heard them scream* once, *when they were being carried into the van. After that, nothing, even though I've been tracking them close enough to hear any calls.*

He could hear something, though – a strange, low buzzing. It filled the interior of the van like a mist. His whiskers twitched. Was there something in the van that shrouded shifter mindspeak?

If so, the situation was worse than he had thought. This wasn't just an opportunistic kidnapping. These people had come here planning to take on shifters.

Jack jumped up into the van. The itching, buzzing sensation that had made his whiskers twitch rose to cover his whole body. Well, if he couldn't talk to the kids, he would have to let his actions speak for him.

<Sorry about this, kids> he said anyway, even though he knew they couldn't hear him. <I know it looks like I'm trying to eat you, but trust me...>

He reached out and grasped the closer of the two cages, inserting his claws between the door and latch and twisting. The steel gave under his grasp and the door popped open. A chocolate-brown bolt of lightning shot under his paw and out of the van. He turned to the second cage. This one held the cat that had hissed at him. It was still skulking in the back of the cage, eyeing him warily.

He eased his claws under the latch of the second cage, the same as he had the first, trying to make his movements as slow and un-threatening as possible. Since he was essentially flexing six-inch-long talons through the bars of the cage, he wasn't sure how effective that was. The hinges were just beginning to give when he heard a sharp *pop* and a stinging sensation down his side.

He wrenched the door the rest of the way off and spun around, growling. The driver was standing ten feet away, aiming a handgun directly at him. Jack's first instinct was to jump on his attacker, but then he remembered the scrap of brown fur still trapped behind him. He knew his tiger could probably take a few bullets, but he couldn't risk the driver's shot going wide and hitting either of the children.

Jack backed farther into the van's crawlspace, making sure his body filled the space between the shooter and the second small cat. He snarled, baring his teeth, and the man's hands shook, the barrel of the gun waving erratically from side to side.

Now that he could get a clear look at the driver, Jack confirmed it wasn't de Jager. Which meant the man wasn't working alone.

The driver's mouth moved, as though he was trying to speak but couldn't force the words out. He gulped audibly, then managed to shout: "Stay in the van! Stay there, and nobody needs to get hurt!"

He took one hand off the gun and fumbled in his back pocket.

Jack was about to take advantage of his momentary distraction when a dark shadow dashed out from under the van and launched itself at the man's face. Tiny claws lashed out and drew four lines of blood across his forehead.

Jack tensed. The driver was off-kilter now, but it wouldn't take him long to grab the small cat and hurt it. He had to move now.

He leapt, knocking the gun from their attacker's hand with one heavy paw and pushing him to the ground. The little brown cat fled back under the van. Jack thought he heard a quiet <Yeah!> in the back of his mind.

Whatever had masked their mindspeak before wasn't permanent, then.

He lowered his snout to the fallen driver's face and snarled.

<Scram.>

Maybe the man couldn't hear the words, but he definitely got the message. Jack watched him run down the road toward the motorway until he disappeared.

He had left his gun and phone behind, and a pungent

smell of fear. Jack carefully sniffed the gun. It was loaded, and the safety was off. Trying to move it without using fingers was going to be a bad idea.

Jack stepped away and winced. The man had shot him in the side. The wound stung when he moved, but he couldn't tell if that was bad or not. He tried to twist to look at the bullet wound and hissed in pain.

A soft meow caught his attention. The two cats were huddled together under the van, wide eyes staring at him, ears and tails flicking suspiciously.

<*You remember me, don't you?*> he asked. <*I'm Jack. Toni's … friend. You met me yesterday.*>

<*I was a bit taller then, though*> he finished lamely.

The two cats were completely identical. Small and sleek, with short chocolate-brown fur and shiny blue eyes. He felt an itching sensation at the back of his mind, like someone was talking about him behind his back, and realized that was almost right – except the kids were talking about him right in front of him. They were just aiming their mindspeak so precisely that he couldn't eavesdrop in.

Jack blinked, fighting back a sudden wave of loneliness. Was this something his parents would have taught him how to do, if they had lived longer?

His side ached. He shook his head to dislodge the melancholic thoughts.

<*Lexi, Felix, you have to come with me. Toni is waiting for us back at the campground – she'll be going crazy worrying about you by now.*>

<*Nuh-uh*> piped up a tiny voice. <*She's—*>

Suddenly a blinking light on the ground caught Jack's eye. The driver's phone was lying face-down on the tarmac.

Jack reached out with one paw and then realized just how pointless that would be. He searched inside himself, found his human form, and felt his body begin to shift. His spine and legs twisted, pulling him from all fours onto two feet. The calloused pads of his paws shrunk and stretched into fingers and he shivered as his thick fur receded and the cool night air swept over his bare skin.

Fingers. Good. He snatched up the phone and turned it over. The screen was cracked from top to bottom, but the display was still working. A new text was flashing across the screen.

Ignoring the sound of snickering behind him – if the kids were giggling over seeing his butt they surely couldn't be too traumatised by the kidnapping – he started to swipe the message open, then paused. The roar of a car engine was growing louder. Coming closer.

Jack tensed, concentrating with all his senses. If the driver had alerted backup—

It's her.

Relief washed over Jack as his shifter senses told him Toni was the one behind the wheel. He couldn't have explained how he knew it was her. She was too far away to see, hear or smell, but he knew without a doubt that the car racing up the road contained her, and only her. The shifter part of his mind was sure of it.

The human part of his mind remembered to jump to the side of the road before the car came haring around the bend.

Brakes screeched as Toni forced the speeding car to a stop just past the crashed van. She leapt out of the car, eyes wide. "Jack – where are—"

Jack watched as her gaze went slightly unfocused, and he

realized the twins were mindspeaking with her. Her expression went from fear, to relief, to shock. "You're both okay, though, right? Come here and let me look at you."

The two small cats darted out from under the van and smooched around her legs. Toni picked them up one at a time and hugged them tight. Jack could just make out tears welling in her eyes before she blinked them back, mumbling reassuring nothings to the children.

Was she a cat shifter, like them? He couldn't wait to find out. To talk to her properly, honestly, not hiding anything any longer.

He was also starting to feel the cold.

He cleared his throat. Toni glanced over at him and went pink as he attempted to mime his predicament.

"There are some blankets in the trunk. Key's in the ignition," she said quickly, though without averting her gaze. "Grab some for the kids, too, please?"

Jack popped the trunk and easily found the pile of blankets. They were thick, woollen blankets, the sort of thing you might have around for emergency picnics. He wrapped one around his waist and passed the other two to Toni, who dropped them neatly over the two kittens' heads.

"All right, kids. In your own time." She turned back to Jack, arms crossed defensively over her chest. "Jack..."

"I—" Jack began, and then reality caught up with him. This was no time for lengthy explanations. He had to get them all somewhere safe, where they could figure out what the hell was going on and how to deal with de Jager and his crew.

"You can't go back to the campground," he said in the end, stumbling over the words. "I've got a house in the forest. You'll be safer there. Please. I can look after you there."

He watched her think it over, eyes flickering as she took in the scene around them. The crashed van with claw-marks on the back door and open cages inside. The two kids, in human shape now, huddled in their blankets. And him, in the middle of it all and – yes – bleeding slightly from the wound on his hip.

"I'll explain on the way," he said to fill the silence.

"Good idea," she said at last, setting her jaw. "You drive."

NINE

TONI

Jack told her what had happened: the cages, the driver with a gun. His voice was calm, but he was gripping the wheel so tightly his knuckles were bone-white. When he finished, Toni felt worse than when she'd had no idea what was going on.

He shared her suspicion that de Jager – and however many men he had with him – had come to Silver Forest with the express purpose of hunting shifters. And they had the technology to do so. They could detect mindspeak, and they could silence it, which meant they could find shifters and prevent them from calling for help, or warning others.

They'd almost succeeded. Jack had saved the twins, but the driver had escaped. How long until he reported back to de Jager? How long until they struck again?

Lexi and Felix were sitting in the back, wrapped in their blankets. Toni kept a worried eye on them as Jack drove past the campground and on to a long gravel road. They had both looked very pale when they first shifted back, and were still unnaturally quiet and still in the car. But Toni could feel them talking to each other just out of her mental hearing, and while the sensation of their secret mindspeak usually set her on edge, this time she was glad of it. They might not be ready to talk to her, but they were talking to each other. That was something, at least.

To be honest, if they had started asking her questions about what had happened, she wasn't sure how she would answer. What had happened was so terrifying she could barely think about it; her mind edged around the thought as though it would burn if she got too close. How could she talk to them about it without terrifying them even more?

Then there was Jack. Jack, who had stolen her heart the moment she met him – and, hell, that had only been yesterday! Jack, who had been so wonderful, who had romanced her as though she was the most beautiful woman in the world. Who...

Had disappeared into the night after the van that held Lexi and Felix. Had run and somehow caught up with a speeding vehicle, and rescued them.

Jack, who clearly *wasn't* telling her everything. But she had a pretty strong suspicion what he might be leaving out.

Catching up with a speeding van? His clothes all mysteriously disappearing between him running off and her catching up with him? Those claw marks on the van doors?

She'd have to be an idiot not to figure it out.

Jack was a shifter. Something big, and powerful.

She could feel the unsaid conversation hanging in the air. No, not just the conversation: The Conversation. Capitalized.

～

They drove on through the forest for about an hour, winding along the narrow road under the trees. Toni could see Jack keeping watch on their surroundings as he drove, and was reassured by the thought that, with their shifter powers, either he or the twins would likely pick up on anyone lurking in the shadows. As they went deeper into the forest the flat ground gave way to rolling hills, all covered in thick, old-growth trees.

Suddenly they turned a corner and the forest fell away to reveal a wide road leading up to what Toni could only imagine was Jack's house. The sight was enough to drive the worries from her mind, if only momentarily.

So this is the house that Jack built, she thought, too awed to make the joke out loud.

She knew his family used to live in the area, so she had been expecting an old building, a stately wooden pile gone slightly creaky with age. Instead, the house in front of her was slickly modern. There was wood, yes, but only as an accent to floor-to-ceiling windows that caught the light from the car's headlights and scattered it back across the ground.

Toni could only see one storey from the road, and the building's flat roof made it look as though the house was sinking into the landscape – like it was a great glass-and-wood creature just resting in the forest, not impinging upon it. Simple steps led up to a wide, open deck; Toni could imagine what it would be like to relax there on a hot day, surrounded by the serenity of the woods. If only they were arriving in difference circumstances ... if only everything had been different.

"I'm sorry about the state of the place," Jack said, his voice tinged with embarrassment. "I've only been back in the country for a few weeks, and I haven't exactly made weeding a priority..."

Toni refocused her gaze to the open ground in front of the beautiful house. Maybe it had been a proper lawn at some point, but the forest was taking over, sending out creeping ferns and wild bursts of colorful flowers to recolonize the space. She smiled. "I'm glad you didn't. Give me a little wilderness over sculpted gardens any day."

Jack pulled in to a covered carport hidden along the side of the house. He paused before opening the door. "I'll check the house first. I haven't had any alerts from the security system, but just in case..."

Toni nodded and watched as he moved silently to the front door. For a few minutes she couldn't see or hear anything from inside the house, then a light switched on and she heard Jack calling out for her and the kids to come in.

Lexi wriggled eagerly out of the car and then paused and turned back, waiting for Toni and Felix to catch up before she went any further. Toni felt her heart sink. She had always wished the kids would be less of a handful, less taken to haring off out of sight the moment her back was turned, but now all she wanted was for them to feel safe enough to be able to do just that.

Not just to *feel* safe enough, she corrected herself, shivering. For them to *be* safe enough. For them not to have to worry about anything like this happening again.

She wrapped her arms around the twins' shoulders and led them up to the house. Jack was standing silhouetted in the orange light of the entranceway; in that moment, he, and the house behind him, seemed like the only warm and safe place in the entire forest. Toni hurried forward.

"Come on in." Jack ushered them inside, then pressed some buttons on a control panel beside the entranceway. The door shut and locked behind Toni with a reassuring *thunk*. Jack's hands flew over the controls. "I'm just activating the privacy settings. We'll be able to see out, but no one outside can see in the windows. They won't even be able to tell if the lights are on."

"They'll see the car outside, though," Toni pointed out.

Jack raised one eyebrow and, with a flourish, pressed one final button. A mechanical hum filled the air and Toni looked out the nearest window to see a wall descending down the side of the carport, hiding the car from view.

She whistled. "Nice."

<*'m hungry*> whispered a small voice at the edge of Toni's mind.

Toni ruffled Felix's hair and looked across at Jack.

"Any chance of something to eat before I put these two to bed?"

"Absolutely," Jack replied, leading the way farther into the house. "I'll grab some of my old clothes for the kids, and I'll put on some food while you all get washed up."

Toni couldn't stop her eyes from flicking downwards when he said the word 'clothes' because, of course, he still wasn't actually wearing any. And while the blankets from Toni's car might be sufficiently robe-like when wrapped around an eight-year-old, they didn't exactly provide full coverage of Jack's muscular frame.

Her eyes lingered over the strong lines of Jack's back as he showed them to the bathroom. Lingered – and then turned away, guiltily.

He must think I'm a shifter. How could he not, after

tonight? And after everything that had happened that afternoon ... what if he thought that she was – that they were...?

She shook her head. There was enough going on already. She would have to admit it to him eventually, that she was just a normal human. But not yet. *Please, not yet*, she begged silently, though she wasn't sure who she was begging.

No.

Toni had heard her mom and dad talk about how sometimes their cats would talk to them, but Toni was no shifter. It was her own voice she heard in her head. After all, there was no one else in there to be the voice of reason.

I have to tell him. Soon. I can't lie to him about something like this – even lying by omission. It has to be tonight.

Then Jack spoke, and Toni realized they had stopped walking.

"Here we are," he said, opening a door. Toni fumbled with the bathroom light switch, and gasped as soft light illuminated a surprisingly large room.

"Wooooow!" cried Lexi and Felix in unison. Toni didn't blame them. The bathroom was luxuriously fitted out and, Toni realized with a strange swooping feeling in her stomach, probably the size of her entire apartment back in the city.

Felix and Lexi leapt into the room, investigating it inch by inch like the curious cats they were. They peered into cupboards, ran their fingers along the smooth edges of the floor-to-ceiling marble tiling, and pressed every button they could see and reach – which was a lot of buttons.

As lights and taps flicked on and off, Toni glanced back out into the corridor to see that Jack had disappeared.

She squared her shoulders. Right. This was her chance to

talk to him while the kids were occupied, and before she had a chance to wuss out.

Toni retraced her steps through the house. The house was bigger than it had looked from the outside – all that glass made it reflect so much of the forest, the actual size of the building was camouflaged – but it was surprisingly easy to find her way around.

She eventually found Jack in a mudroom at the other end of the house, bent over a low counter. A battered first-aid kit sat on the bench in front of him. Dried blood was flaking from his skin as he tried to twist to look at the wound in his side. Dried blood – and fresh.

"Let me look at that," Toni demanded. Her voice came out more harshly than she had intended, but her whole body was itching with displeasure at the thought of Jack in pain. "You'll only injure yourself more if you move around like that."

Jack looked up, his face tight with pain. "Toni, you don't need to—"

"Clearly, I *do*," Toni argued, and pulled the first-aid kit over to herself. She rifled through it and quickly plucked out an antiseptic cream and some sterile gauze. "You're in safe hands with me. I just renewed my Red Cross first aid certificate."

"They teach you about bullet wounds for that?"

"Short answer, no. But they did teach us what to do if someone skewers themselves on a pair of pruning shears, so ... same difference, right?"

Jack chuckled, then winced. "Hah! Ouch."

"Sorry. No more bad jokes."

Toni began to wash away the blood crusted along Jack's side, using soft, gentle strokes. She was relieved to see there was more blood than there was wound. And what wound there was looked several days, rather than several hours, old.

"This isn't looking too bad," she announced, reaching for a sterile bandage. "The bullet must have just grazed you. I can *see* exactly *where* it grazed you, actually, and trust me, it's pretty gross. But it's not bleeding anymore." She secured the bandage, and paused. "Quick healer, huh?"

"Always have been," Jack replied, his voice soft. "My family, too. Just like you."

"Just like me," Toni echoed. *No, wait,* she thought at Jack turned to look at her. A thousand words bubbled up in her brain, and tripped over on her tongue.

"Now let me look after you," Jack said. Toni frowned, confused – and the expression stung her face.

"Ow. Oh, right. My major case of roadburn," she babbled.

"Fast healing is good for some things, but it makes cleaning wounds a hell of a priority," Jack said, gently tilting Toni's face into the light and dabbing at her cheekbone with a dampened cloth. "You don't want to sleep on it and wake up to find your skin has grown back over a fistful of gravel."

Toni tried to smile without wrinkling her face – and the graze – too much. "Tell me about it. Ellie – my sister – spent five years trying to get her ear piercings to stick. They'd just grow over each time. Once, they actually grew back *over* her earrings."

"You never bothered?" Jack's fingers brushed Toni's naked earlobe.

Of course she hadn't. After her sister's experiences, Toni hadn't wanted to try experimenting with piercings. She didn't want to risk having them stick, and become another difference between her and her shifter family.

Jack finished with her cheek and moved on to the graze on her forearm. An image flashed up in Toni's mind, as though she was looking at the two of them from above – the two of them, together, dressing their wounds after fighting to save the two children. A day ago, neither of them known the other existed; but today, they were a team. A unit.

Almost a family.

And, like a family, secrets boiled under their seemingly unified exterior.

Toni took a deep breath.

"Jack, I have to—"

"Tiger," he said, almost at the same time.

Their eyes met, and a relieved smile burst across Jack's face.

"God, it feels so good to actually say it!" He laughed. "I've been standing here like an idiot, trying to figure out how to say it. And before, in the car..."

He stepped forward and swept Toni into his arms in the same movement.

"I'm a tiger," he repeated, his words muffled in Toni's hair. "It matches, right? A big cat. Bigger than normal tigers, even, not that I found that out until I'd been shifting for a decade."

"Right," Toni mumbled. She could feel herself wavering, enfolded safely in his arms. It would be so easy to put off telling him...

She steeled herself. "Jack, I—"

"... I know not all shifters' animals are bigger than the normal versions – like your family, right? I saw the kids. No one could tell they weren't regular cats. And..." Jack had been talking, quickly, breathlessly, as though all the words he hadn't said for the last few hours were rushing out at once. But when he felt Toni stiffen, he paused.

"Is everything all right?"

He loosened his arms around Toni, his hands slipping down to hold her gently by the waist. She looked grimly up at him.

"Jack ... Felix and Lexi are cats, yes, like their parents. And they're normal-sized. But, Jack, I—"

<Auntie Toni!>

Toni could have screamed. Of all the rotten timing—

But as quickly as her irritation had flared, it disappeared. The voice – Lexi's – hadn't been scared, but it echoed with anxiety.

"You should go," Jack said, and she realized he'd heard as well. She was surprised; usually the twins were more careful about keeping their shouts family-only. "We can talk later," Jack added, lifting one hand to gently touch the edge of her grazed cheek. "Once the kids are settled in properly."

"Yes," Toni said absently, as inside her, her better self fought with her selfish side. Quickly, before she could change her mind, she grabbed Jack's hand from her cheek and kissed it.

"We'll talk later," she promised. "And Jack – you know I, I care about you, right?"

She ran out of the room, before it became obvious just how much of an understatement those words were.

The bathroom was full of steam, bubbles, and puddles.

"Kids?" Toni called as she knocked on the door. "Everything okay?"

"Y-yeah," admitted Lexi guiltily. She was perched on the edge of the bathroom counter, wrapped in a towel and studiously filling the marble sink with frothy bubbles. Felix was sitting in a pile of bubbles in front of her. Neither child would meet Toni's eye. "I just, you know..."

"...just wanted to make sure I was still around," Toni finished. "I understand."

"And that you would come back," Lexi added, her voice so quiet Toni could barely hear it. Toni felt a pit open in the bottom of her stomach.

"Sweetie, you know I'll always come as fast as I can," she managed to say, wrapping her arms around her niece's slight form. Lexi wriggled around and hugged Toni back.

For about thirty seconds. Then Lexi flapped at Toni's arms until she let go, and grabbed a heap of bubbles from the sink. Toni watched, waiting for the other shoe to fall, as her niece piled bubbles on top of her nephew until the black-haired boy almost disappeared under a pile of froth.

At the other end of the bathroom, the shower was still running. Keeping one eye on the twins – still not entirely trusting their apparent change of mood – Toni ducked underneath the hot cascade of water long enough to rinse off the worst of the day's sweat and dirt.

It was like standing in a tropical rainstorm, hot water sheeting down from the ceiling and swirling around her feet. She bent her head forward and let the water wash over her neck and shoulders, pummeling her stress away.

When she looked at herself in the mirror, the graze on her cheek seemed far smaller than its sting made it feel, though that may have just been the steam obscuring her vision. She dabbed the broken skin carefully with the corner of her towel and decided to leave it to air-dry.

At least it wasn't bleeding at all, since Jack had cleaned it. *Jack.*

Toni's mind whirled. Looking at herself in the mirror, she could see her face change even at just the thought of him – her cheeks pink, her pupils huge and black.

She groaned and let her head drop forward until her forehead *clonked* onto glass. What she'd seen in the mirror? It was the same expression she'd seen on Jack's face. When he looked at her.

She couldn't fool herself any longer. And she couldn't let Jack be fooled, either. If he thought she was a shifter – if he thought, God forbid, after this afternoon, that they were *meant* to be together, that she could be his m—

She couldn't even think the word.

Like so much else in her life, *that* – the m-word – was something Toni knew she couldn't have. It was a shifter thing; she wasn't a shifter; it didn't take a genius to do the math.

It didn't help that every new thing she learnt about Jack confirmed that he was a good guy, the genuine article. He'd run to save the twins without question, and brought them all back here to his home, despite the fact that doing so could mean putting himself in harm's way.

And it wasn't just the big things. While Toni was busy glaring at herself in the mirror, human foam-volcano Felix had cracked the door open to discover Jack had left a pile of clothes outside. And the house was beginning to fill with the most delicious smells...

He was the perfect man. And she had to tell him that she was far from the perfect woman for him.

Toni pulled an oversized shirt over her head, trying as she did so not to think of it as *Jack's shirt*, of it sliding over his shoulders and chest. It was long enough for her to belt it into a shirtdress.

The adult-sized shirts and sweaters were long enough on the kids to be tunics, and the hems flapped against their knees as they followed their noses to the kitchen.

"Food's up!" Jack called happily as Toni walked through the door. Like the rest of the house, the kitchen combined cutting-edge equipment with a focus on comfort. Jack was standing behind a tall bench, ladling steaming pasta onto plates. The twins were already scrambling up onto two of the stools that lined the bench, eyes fixed on the food. Toni walked up and took a seat beside them.

He looks like he belongs there, Toni thought. *Like family.*

She shook her head. That was the *opposite* of the sort of thing she needed to be thinking, right now.

Jack was smiling at her, though, and she couldn't stop her own lips turning up in response.

"May I present my specialty dish: pasta with a sauce of whatever cheeses I could find in the fridge," Jack announced modestly. "For the first course, pasta. For the second, pasta again. And so forth until you're all either full, or we run out of food."

Toni's stomach rumbled and she realized how long it had been since that light lunch on the riverside. She wound her fork around a strand of spaghetti and lifted it to her mouth.

"Jack, this is delicious. Carbs and cheese, the best thing

after a..." she glanced sideways at the kids and decided not to say *scary* or *terrifying* "...busy day."

She tucked in as Jack pulled up a stool on the other side of the bench. Beside her, Lexi and Felix attacked their meals with gusto. Toni felt a tight knot in her stomach begin to relax as she watched the kids enjoy the meal.

A blinking light further down the bench caught her attention.

"Is that your phone?" she asked around a mouthful of savory sauce. "It looks like you've got a message."

Jack frowned and grabbed the phone. "That's – it's nothing. Nothing important." He stuck the phone in his pocket and turned to the twins. "You two want seconds?"

"Yes!" two voices cried happily.

The shower – or at least the bubbles – and the meals might have gone some way toward restoring the children's sense of security, but the moment Toni suggested it was time for them to go to bed, that went out the window. Jack had made up a bed in a spare room for the kids but they clung to Toni, silently refusing to move. Toni couldn't blame them.

In the end she and Jack hauled the blankets from the spare bed to the living room, and built a nest on one of the sofas. Toni sat between her niece and nephew, while Jack curled into a large leather armchair across from them.

Toni brushed her fingers gently over Lexi's forehead. Neither of the twins was talking much, though she could feel the soft buzz of private mindspeak at the edge of her own mind. She wasn't surprised; the twins had always talked big things over between themselves before involving anyone else, even before they were old enough *to* talk to anyone else.

Slowly, the buzz receded, and the two children's breathing slowed and deepened as they drifted off to sleep.

"Will they be all right?" Jack had a searching look in his eyes, and it was all Toni could do to stop her own million questions from flooding out all at once. She took a deep breath.

"I don't know," she said softly, not wanting to wake them. She looked down at Felix curled up beside her, his hands tucked up under his chin. "Nothing like this has ever happened to them before. I don't know whether that means this will hit them badly, or whether ... I don't know much about psychology. Or anything about it, really. But if they don't understand how much danger they were really in ... maybe that can make it easier for them to cope with it?"

"Maybe," Jack agreed, but there was still a tension in his body. His eyes were flickering gold in the firelight. Toni knew what that meant, now: his tiger was close to the surface.

"I—" she began, then coughed, her throat dry. She tried again. "I was thinking ... if they are traumatized, would it help them at all to transform? I know Ellie, my sister, when she was younger, she would sober up after a night on the town by transforming. Shifting helps her metabolize the alcohol, or something. And..."

She tried to claw up memories from college, from the health sciences classes she had taken with her vet friend Roxie before switching majors. "Sometimes trauma can have to do with the brain producing particular chemicals, can't it? Is that a thing? If shifting can help metabolize alcohol, maybe it can help reduce other mental effects, too."

A line appeared between Jack's eyebrows. Toni licked her lips, suddenly nervous.

"I have to ask you. I can't answer the question myself. Because I don't *know*. All I know is, is what Ellie's told me, or my parents, the rest of my family. I'm not a shifter, Jack," and oh, it was so hard to keep her voice steady, not to disturb the kids. "I know there are more important things we have to talk about, like whatever the hell de Jager is up to, but – I can't let you think I'm something I'm not."

She couldn't look at him. She couldn't bear the thought of seeing the shock and disappointment in his eyes as he realized she wasn't who he thought she was. *What* he thought she was.

"Toni..."

She squeezed her eyes shut, but a tear still managed to escape. "Don't, Jack. I know it's not what – I'm sorry. I should have said something earlier."

She felt, rather than heard, him stand up and walk slowly over to her, then the puff of air as he knelt down. When he spoke, his voice was gentle.

"The alcohol thing is true enough. I don't know if it would work with other brain chemistry, though. I don't know the science behind it, but personally..." He sighed. "Things stick with you regardless of what shape you're in."

He laid a hand on Toni's knee. "Or what shape *you* are. Toni, darling ... I thought you were human when I first started falling for you. When my tiger first noticed you. It doesn't change anything."

Toni hung her head. "Of course it does. Can't you see? You just said it—" Her voice began to waver and she realized she couldn't do this. Not here. Slowly, carefully, she manoeuvred her way off the sofa, away from the warm bundle of blankets and the sleeping children.

She pulled Jack with her out of the room and shut the door behind them both. He watched her, silent, his eyes golden and alert.

Toni ran her hands through her hair, despairing. "You said it yourself. Your tiger noticed me. I can't – I can never do that for you. I don't have a tiger, or a cat, or *anything*. I'm just *me*."

Jack was still watching her, and she could feel it, the magnetic pull between their bodies. A sob burst out of her and she relented, let that force pull her in to his arms. He held her with one arm around her waist, the other buried deep in her still-damp hair.

He smelled like the forest, pine and rich soil over his own deep, masculine scent. And below that, she could sense his tiger, powerful, lean, strength in every coiled muscle.

"You're all I need, Toni," Jack whispered. "Just you."

"It's not enough," Toni insisted. "*I'm* not enough. I never have been. Didn't today prove that? De Jager took the twins, and there was nothing I could do."

She pulled away from his embrace, even though every inch of her was wailing at her to stay. "I'm not who you need me to be, Jack. I'm not strong enough, or powerful enough. I can't *help*. We need to figure out how to stop de Jager, but what part can I play in any plan we come up with? The only thing I can think of to do is call my family, but even my *phone* doesn't work!"

The words tumbled out of her like bitter knives, all facing inwards. It was as though a dam had burst inside her, and years of insecurity were flooding out.

Jack reached out to her again and she thrust his hand away.

"Don't, Jack. I – I can't." *I can't be with you. I can't be with you, and watch you realize how pathetic I am. Watch you always one step ahead, faster, stronger, better.*

Watch you leave me behind.

He stood back, pushing his hands deep into his pockets. Toni could feel his confusion, his need to touch her, to comfort her. But his touch couldn't comfort her now, only distract her. The pain would still be there, waiting underneath.

At last he seemed to come to a decision.

"Follow me," he said. "I want to show you something."

He led her to the mudroom where they had dressed each other's wounds, and unlocked a cabinet.

"I don't want you to feel unsafe here. It may not look like it, but this building is reinforced throughout. You'd need a tank to get in the front door, and the windows are bulletproof, as well as one-directional blackout. That means that we can see out, but no one can see in. You're safe here. And if this makes you feel safer..."

Toni gasped as something gleamed oily gray in the back of the cupboard. A handgun.

"The man who kidnapped Lexi and Felix dropped this. He took two shots with it, but the rest of the clip's still in there." He reached out, then seemed to reconsider, and instead dropped the key to the cabinet in Toni's hand. "It's here if you need it."

Toni's fingers closed automatically over the key. Then she shook her head and placed it carefully on the cabinet.

"I don't know how to use that," she said quietly.

"I thought – if you felt you didn't have to depend on me to protect you..." Jack sighed, bowing his head.

The thought of shooting a person with the same gun that had left that gash in Jack's side made her stomach churn. But the alternative...

"I'd be more likely to hurt someone than to help. Well," she said, miserably, "hurt someone who I didn't *mean* to hurt, I mean..."

"I understand." Jack shook his head. "Well, you'll be safe here, anyway."

"With you," Toni murmured.

And that was the problem, wasn't it? He was a tiger shifter, strong and powerful not only in his shifted form but his human body, as well. And what was she? Just a human, who wasn't even confident in the one body she did have.

Toni felt a lump grow in her throat.

"I'd better go and check on the kids," she said hurriedly, and turned to leave. As she reached the door, Jack caught hold of her arm.

"Toni – you may not want to hear it now, but I meant what I said. I'm not going to give up on you."

Too late, Toni thought bitterly. *I've already given up on myself.*

TEN
JACK

A HOT WIND RUSTLED THE TREETOPS, SENDING SHADOWS waving across the star-studded sky. A dark shape, rust-colored stripes barely visible in the moonlight, padded softly toward the treeline.

Jack hesitated just before the edge of the trees, looking back at his house – no, his home. Now that Toni was there, how could it be anything else?

Even if he wasn't there.

Toni had exposed her secret to him tonight, ironic though it was that someone would have to admit to *not* being a shifter.

More than that, she'd revealed her true secret, her deepest fear: that being a shifter meant she would never be good enough. The revelation made Jack's heart ache.

But it was what he'd left unsaid that made his gut clench with guilt.

Jack bit down on the roll of clothing he was carrying in his mouth, until he could just feel the hard surface of the van driver's phone through the fabric.

He should have told her about it. Should have said something when she saw it on the kitchen counter – and hell, how stupid had he been, to leave it out in plain sight? Either of the kids might have grabbed it and read through the messages.

Those messages made it clear that the kids hadn't been de Jager's primary target. Jack had had his suspicions even before he found the phone; why else would the man show up here after all these years?

The van driver, de Jager's assistant, had grabbed the kids just because they were there. A little bonus for the boss. Jack was the real target.

Which was why he was leaving Toni and the kids safely hidden behind layers of high-tech security, and venturing out into the woods under cover of darkness.

He couldn't risk leading the hunters straight to them again. So instead, he was taking the fight to the hunters. And although his stomach crawled with guilt at leaving Toni behind, he knew he couldn't bear to put Toni and the children in danger again.

Jack huffed quietly and turned back toward the forest. In a second, he was loping silently between the trees, his location fixed in his mind like the North Star.

The phone didn't just have messages on it. It had contacts, plans – and maps.

De Jager had made his base at the abandoned mines deep within the park. It was no wonder the rangers hadn't found him. The mines were strictly no-access, due to how dangerous they were. Any normal campers would have steered well clear.

Which was good, because that meant there wouldn't be any stray passers-by to see Jack's planned rendezvous with de Jager.

That man – no, that *creature* had killed dozens of wild animals out of rage at the fact that big game hunting was about to be made illegal. If he was hunting shifters...

Jack might not have close connections to shifter society, but he knew enough to understand what really made shifters frightened. Shifters needed to keep their powers secret, so it was impossible for them to go to the authorities if anyone was harming them in a way that touched on their shifter natures. If someone was hunting shifters – hell, there were plenty of places in the world where big-game hunting was still legal. And regular hunting, and trapping, culling, vermin control...

When a shifter died, they stayed in whatever shape they held when they drew their last breath. And no human court on Earth would prosecute a murder if the victim looked for all the world like a dumb animal.

Keeping low to the ground, Jack zeroed in on his target. De Jager's last message said he'd be at the meeting point at eight; Jack would be there by six. He could lie in wait for hours if need be.

And when de Jager arrived...

Golden eyes glinted in the moonlight. When de Jager arrived, Jack and he had some unfinished business to take care of.

ELEVEN
TONI

Sun was streaming in through the living-room window by the time Toni woke up. After fleeing from Jack the night before, she had returned to the blanket nest on the sofa, acutely aware of how anxious the twins had been the last time she'd gone out of their sight. But now, even with the twins huddled beside her, the house felt ... empty.

"Jack?"

Toni nudged her way out of the blankets, and sleepy yawns followed her as she walked out into the corridor. She poked her head into the kitchen, then knocked on the bathroom door. No Jack.

A flight of stairs led down to the bedrooms. This had confused Toni last night, until she realized that the apparently single-level house was set into the side of the hill, with another story dropping down the side from the entry-level ground floor. She'd helped Jack gather blankets and pillows from a spare bedroom, and knew Jack's own room must be down there, too.

She quickly checked the stripped spare room, then hesitated at the next, closed door.

"Jack?"

There was no response to her tentative knock. Biting her lip, she opened the door.

There was no mistaking that this was the master bedroom. Jack's room. The floor was covered with a thick carpet the color of pine needles, and floor-to-ceiling windows let the morning sun in to wash over creamy white walls. The furniture was all made of the same heavy wood, polished to buttery smoothness. A king-sized bed was positioned to catch the view.

But there was no sign of Jack.

Toni let out her breath. She had to accept the obvious: he wasn't here.

So, where had he gone?

Toni gnawed her bottom lip. She remembered the phone she had seen on the bench the night before, the phone Jack had hidden after she mentioned it. Why hadn't she pressed him about it then?

The gun might not have been the only thing Jack picked up from the van crash site. If Jack had the driver's phone, he might have been able to track down the hunters somehow. But if he'd left without leaving a note...

Toni's whole body went cold. She hadn't known Jack long, but she was positive he wouldn't deliberately re-traumatize the children by disappearing on them. Wherever he'd gone, he must have thought he would be back before the rest of them woke up.

"Auntie Toni?"

Toni hurried back to the foot of the stairs and looked up at Felix. The dark-haired boy was rubbing his eyes sleepily.

"Hey, kiddo," she said, trying to smile. "Where's your sister?"

<I'm here> came Lexi's voice around the corner, soon followed by her four-footed self. Lexi jumped effortlessly on to her brother's shoulder and sat there with her tail wrapped around his neck for balance.

"What's the matter, Auntie Toni?" Felix's voice was insistent. Toni wiped the back of her hand across her face. Were her emotions that obvious?

"Jack went out on a, an errand earlier this morning," she said at last. "He meant to be back by now, but..."

The two children looked at each other. <Mr. Silver is really tough> Lexi began, <but...>

Felix completed her sentence. "The man in the van had a gun," he said. "He shot Mr. Silver before he made him drop it and run away."

Toni frowned. "Who said anything about him going after the hunters?" she said quickly, then sighed. So much for hiding her suspicions from the kids to stop them worrying.

<...obviously gone after the hunters, oh my god> muttered Lexi, just loud enough that Toni could pick up the words.

"Dammit," Toni muttered under her own breath. She turned away from the stairs. The whole back of the house was covered in floor-to-ceiling windows, just like the master bedroom, giving a vertigo-inducing view over the forest. "Where are you, Jack?"

She put her palms to the cool glass, and let her forehead fall to rest between them. It was like looking down into an ocean of green, waving branches. Farther out, the solid mass of green was broken by rocky outcrops and the winding curve of the river, and beyond that, the rising hills as forest gave way to mountains.

And Jack was out there somewhere.

Where?

Toni closed her eyes, concentrating. She'd felt a – a sort of magnetic attraction to Jack ever since they'd met. At the time, she had put it down to his incredible hotness, but after last night's revelation that he was a tiger shifter...

Toni let the tiny ray of hope direct her thoughts. If that pull toward Jack was something to do with his shifter nature, and her own shifter heritage, could she call on that now? After all, she thought, flexing her hands, she knew now that she shared her family's healing powers. Why not this?

And ... now that she thought about it, this wouldn't be the first time she had used that gravitational pull as a sort of magical homing device. After Jack had run off into the night, Toni had sprinted to her car, wondering how she would ever manage to catch up with the van, let alone find Jack wherever he ended up. But as she had buckled in and taken the wheel, a calm certainty had descended upon her. She had known, somehow, that she would find Jack only a few miles away. It had been as though an invisible ribbon connected them, and all she had to do to find him was follow it.

It had worried her, how this new shifter power she had developed seemingly skipped over the most important missing persons to zero in on ... well, a fantastic lay ... but she had pushed that concern aside last night. With her new knowledge of Jack's shifter status, and the "m" word hovering on her mental horizon, she pushed it aside even *more* firmly now. Her new power was going to point her right to the very man she wanted to find. That was the important thing.

Toni focused. There it was. The same magnetic pull she had felt the first time she met Jack, and yesterday, on their ride along the river, and on that frantic car chase through the night. A gentle, insistent force, as natural as gravity, or a river's current.

And at the other end of it: Jack.

With her eyes closed, Toni felt the connection to his presence as though it were a tangible thing, a rope that she could pull herself along and reach out to touch him. Toni could almost believe that if she breathed in, she would be able to smell him; that if she leaned forward, she would feel the heat of his skin on hers. Around her, she could sense the cool shadows of the thickly wooded forest, and hear the murmur of leaves brushed by the wind. There was a strange, chemical tang in the air and the soil. She was standing on two legs at the edge of a clearing. And she wasn't alone.

Toni opened her eyes and swayed. A wave of light-headedness struck her, and her heart was racing as though she had just run up a flight of stairs.

What was that? she wondered silently, rubbing her forehead. For a moment, it had been as though she really had transported out into the forest. And even now, with her consciousness firmly back in her own body, she could still feel the cool touch of the forest at the edge of her senses.

And Jack...

Jack was in trouble.

Toni reeled. The thought was like a physical blow. Somehow, she was sure beyond a doubt that it wasn't just speculation.

"Auntie Toni? Are you okay?"

Felix had crept down the stairs to join her while she'd been concentrating. He stood beside her and they both stared out across the seemingly endless expanse of trees.

Toni put her arm out to stroke Lexi and pat Felix's shoulder.

"I – I need to go find Jack," she said unsteadily. Then, with more certainty, "And there is *no way* you two are coming with me."

Throw herself into danger? That was one thing. But after last night, she would die before letting de Jager come within sniffing distance of the kids ever again.

"Right," she said, her brain whirring. "Here's the plan..."

As Toni drove along the rutted forest road, she could feel the connection between her and Jack grow stronger. It was as though she were a compass, and he the magnetic north.

Of course, compasses were useful if you could travel as the crow flies, but what Toni really needed was a map. Her connection to Jack was tugging her deeper into forest, but Toni was driving in the opposite direction. She knew she didn't have many outdoors skills, but she knew enough to understand how stupid it would be to strike out into the wilderness with no idea where she was going.

She wouldn't be any help to Jack if she just blindly followed their bond and fell head-first into a hidden ravine or sinkhole. Finding her way along the winding tracks would take longer, but be much safer.

For that, she needed a map. And she knew just the person for that.

Toni caught sight of Karen by the reception hut and screeched the car to a halt. The connection between her and Jack was almost a physical hurt now, as though distancing herself from him had stretched it tight. She gritted her teeth and forced herself to get out of the car, even as all her senses were screaming for her to turn around and race back into the trees.

"Karen!"

The blonde woman turned, surprise on her face. She had been wheeling two mountain bikes to lean against the building. One of them fell over as she hurried toward Toni.

"Toni! What—"

Toni cut her off before she could ask any awkward questions. "Karen, I need a favor. Do you have a map of the forest? With all the paths marked out on it?"

"There should be some in the cabin here, but—" Karen's voice trailed off as Toni rushed past her. "Toni, is everything okay? Jack got in touch last night to let us know you'd found the kids and to call off the search, but are you all right?"

"I'm fine. Jack..." Toni was about to explain that Jack had gone to confront the would-be kidnapper, but the words died on her tongue. How much did Karen know about her friend? Toni didn't doubt that if the meeting with de Jager went south – and the sick feeling in her stomach told her the odds of that were good – Jack would transform. If Toni involved any other non-shifters, what were the chances one of them might attack Jack, by mistake?

No. She couldn't risk it. She would do this herself.

The weight of the handgun in her pack was cold against

her back: a last resort against a situation she didn't want to imagine.

"The maps are here," said Karen, opening a drawer in one of the registration desks. "We're here, and north's that way. You can generally orient it by the mountains, but here's a compass, anyway."

She looked hard into Toni's face. "I can tell something's wrong, Toni. Look ... I know we don't know each other very well, but you're a friend of Jack's, so I hope you believe you can trust me to help, whatever it is."

Toni clenched her fists as a wariness that wasn't quite her own prickled the back of her neck.

"There is one thing you can do," she said. She searched the desk for a pen, and then scribbled two phone numbers on a scrap of paper. "This is my sister Ellie's number, and her husband, Werther. Felix and Lexi's parents. I haven't been able to get through to them from here in the camping ground, but if you could try..."

Both women's eyes fell on the cut phone line behind the desk.

"A couple of the rangers are heading into town this morning to pick up some supplies," Karen said. "I'll go with them and get in touch with your relatives."

"Thanks." The twins had Toni's phone, and instructions to keep trying to call their parents until they got through, but Toni figured a backup wouldn't hurt. "If you get through, tell them to get here as fast as they can, and give them directions to Jack's house."

"In the forest? Toni, I—"

"I *really* don't have time to explain, I'm sorry." Toni gasped.

The connection that linked her to Jack had gone taut, as though it was trying to pull her heart out of her chest. "Please, just call them, and tell them to get down here. I've got to go."

She pressed the paper into Karen's hands and ran outside. The bikes against the wall caught her eye, and she realized they were the ones she and Jack had left at the end of the track the night before.

Toni grabbed the sky-blue bike she'd ridden yesterday and slung it in the back of her car. She had no way of knowing whether the roads she was following would be wide enough to fit a car, and much as she disliked cycling, it was a better option than walking or running.

Now that she was moving in the right direction, the tension in Toni's chest eased. The connection between her and Jack gratefully drew her forward as she navigated the roads along the edge of the forest. Eventually, though, even the gravel roads petered out. Toni bunny-hopped to a stop in a pothole, and gritted her teeth.

This was it. She'd traced the best route she could on the map, and this was the biggest road heading anywhere near in the same direction she needed to go. Even so, there was no way she could fit the car down there.

There was nothing else for it. Toni pulled the bike awkwardly from the back of the car and glared at it.

No helmet, she realized belatedly. She couldn't even remember where she had left it. No matter. She slung one leg over and straightened the bike under her. A deep breath, one foot on a pedal, push, scramble to get the other foot into its stirrup – and she was off.

Sort of.

The where-you-look, there-you-go steering method Toni had perfected the day before still worked, though it did mean that if she didn't want to fall into a pothole, she had to pretend they didn't exist.

Not looking at obstacles was something of a difficult ask. Try as she might, Toni found her eyes twitching back and forth between the flat road in front of her wheels and the rocky holes and pits beside her. When the road finally deteriorated into a mud track, she heaved a sigh of relief. At least that would be relatively soft to fall on.

As she rode, the invisible rope anchored in her chest seemed to almost physically pull her forward, driving her on toward Jack. The shocks of fear and tension that had shivered down the connection had faded, now, something she took as a sign she was getting closer. In fact, if she concentrated, she could almost tell—

Toni opened her eyes and just managed to twist the handlebars to keep herself upright before the bike veered off the path. *Stupid!* She could concentrate on riding, or concentrate on her connection with Jack – not both at the same time.

Her hands were sweating on the handlebars. The last thing she needed was to crash before she even got to Jack.

Come on, body. Do this one thing right, please, and I'll never make you get on a bike again.

She pushed on. Even if she didn't concentrate on her connection to Jack, she could tell she was headed in the right direction. The narrow track wound back and forth up a hill; Toni could just see the top of it through the trees.

She wondered what she would see from the top. This area on the map had been blanked out with a big 'DANGER: NO ENTRY' stamp over the top. But the anchor-rope in her heart was leading her straight into it.

Toni gritted her teeth. A few minutes later, legs aching with effort, she crested the ridge. Her breath caught in her throat.

She had thought the raised ground would give her a better view of her surroundings – but not like this. Below her, a land-slide had cleared a patch of the forest of trees, leaving a wide swath of bare dirt. And beyond that, the lush forest gave way to a tangle of rubble and rusting machinery. There must have been some sort of factory out there, she realized. But it must have been shut down decades ago, and now the forest was reclaiming the land, sending out vines and hardy shrubs to help time break down the ruins.

Something gleamed silver in the rust and rubble. A solid-looking 4WD truck was parked up against what remained of a brick wall, barring the way to what Toni realized must be a drivable road, the first she had seen since she abandoned her car. She backed up hurriedly, concealing herself back in the trees along the ridgeline. She couldn't risk being seen.

She had moved just in time. There was another silvery gleam as a car door opened and de Jager stepped out. He was dressed in a light gray suit, completely incongruous given their surroundings. Dark glasses glinted in the sunlight as he surveyed the area, confidence in every inch of his stance.

"Well, Mr. Silver, are you going to show yourself?"

His voice echoed around the clearing. Toni hadn't noticed the birdsong until it disappeared, leaving a hole of silence after de Jager's words faded.

"Really, Mr. Silver, there's no need to keep playing these games. Did you think I wouldn't notice that you incapacitated the rest of my team as they arrived? Actually, I should thank you! Employees are replaceable, but the thrill of the hunt is, I'm sure you'll agree, without comparison!"

Even from her distant hiding place, Toni could see the smile spread over his perfectly tanned face.

She frowned. He may have been smiling, but he didn't appear to be armed. As she watched, he held his arms out wide.

"You know, when your contract first came up, I thought I was losing it. Surely, after all this time, the universe wouldn't line things up so neatly? And yet, here we are."

His grin widened. It was no longer a smile – just teeth.

"As for the other two freaks ... well, that'll make a nice bonus for the boss."

Anger boiled up in Toni's chest. He was talking about the twins! She clenched her fists, imagining smashing them into de Jager's smug, smiling face.

Then her anger turned into horror as another figure stepped out of the shadows under the trees.

"Jack, no," she whispered under her breath. "He's baiting you. Don't fall for it!"

She watched, her heart in her throat, as Jack stalked toward de Jager. He stopped ten feet away from the other man. Toni could see the tension in every inch of his body – hell, she could feel it in her own body, and she was no longer sure whether that was a result of their bond, or just plain fear.

The two men exchanged words, too quietly for Toni to hear them. Jack threw a cell phone to the ground between them – the phone Toni had seen last night.

So it had been from the driver. And whatever Jack had tried to use it for, de Jager had clearly used it against him to set this trap.

Toni felt sick. She had come all this way, but now that she was here, she had no idea what to do. If she revealed herself, she might distract Jack long enough for de Jager to... what?

She supposed he might have a gun, hidden somewhere under his perfectly tailored clothes. He seemed too calm for a man who was completely unarmed.

Then a movement further down the slope caught her eye, and her veins turned to ice.

A little way down the slope from where she stood, sunlight glinted off dark metal. She wasn't the only person hiding in the trees. A man in camo gear knelt behind a stand of brush, completely concealed from the clearing. He held a rifle aimed directly at Jack.

Toni's chest went tight as she pieced the situation together. Jack had left hours ago, and based on what de Jager had just said, he'd probably had time to deal with any of de Jager's men who were in the area when he arrived. But if de Jager knew he was coming ... then he must have sent those men ahead as bait. Lured Jack into a sense of false security, then called in secret backup.

Jack clearly couldn't tell he was in danger, and as a breeze of air raised goose bumps on the backs of her arms, Toni realized why. The wind was in the sniper's favor, blowing his scent, and Toni's, away from his prey.

The three men were almost perfectly lined up. That was probably the only reason Jack was still alive, Toni realized. The sniper wouldn't risk shooting his boss by accident.

"I have a proposal for you, Mr. Silver!" De Jager was

speaking loudly again, his voice carrying across the clearing. "I told you I should thank you for taking out my advance team. After all, there's no fun to a hunt when the field's already been staked out."

"Say what you've got to say," Jack growled. "You know I don't have any interest in your *hunts*."

He spat the last word as though it hurt his mouth.

De Jager regarded him coolly. Toni wanted to jump out, to scream and wave her arms, warn Jack, but even mindspeaking might surprise him too much, give de Jager time to jump away and the sniper time to get that one shot in. She gulped.

"As I said, my contract is only for you. The two kittens were an unexpected bonus. Or they will be when I catch up with them."

Toni could see Jack's fists clench.

"But I can see that distresses you, Mr. Silver. And I'm sure it is distressing. Two children, carried away to who knows where?"

All traces of humor disappeared from his face. They were replaced by a strange expression, as though de Jager was trying to fake compassion, but had no idea what the concept really was.

"Here's the deal, Mr. Silver. I want my bounty, but I want my hunt, too. You give me that, and I'll leave the kittens alone."

Toni held her breath. Her eyes kept darting between the sniper on the slope below her, and the two men standing so close together across the clearing.

"What do you mean?" Jack asked at the same moment as the question passed through Toni's mind.

De Jager shrugged. "I didn't get into this profession for the money, Mr. Silver. I got into it for the game. You give me a good time, and when I haul your carcass to my employer, I won't say a peep about the kids. You can die knowing you're saving their lives."

And, Toni thought, that might have been the truth – except that as he finished speaking, de Jager took a casual step sideways.

Jack hung his head in his hands. Toni's heart went out to him – was already with him – but her brain was on fire.

De Jager was lying. All that rubbish about the hunt was just that: bullshit. This was the same man who'd piled carcass on top of carcass in front of a government building out of sheer spite, so Toni was pretty sure it wasn't any *game* that interested him. Just death.

And if she didn't do something, Jack would be his next victim.

Her thoughts jumped to the gun in her pack, but her hands were shaking so badly she would be more likely to drop the gun than aim and fire it. She could shout, or mindspeak, but if Jack made any sudden moves the man would likely shoot him on the spot.

She could only think of one thing to do.

Heart hammering in her chest, Toni mounted the bike again and let gravity pull her forward and down the other side of the ridge. Wind whipped across her bare face as she gained speed.

Where you look, there you go. Toni kept her eyes locked on her target: the man with the gun.

If she had had time to think about what she was doing, Toni never would have gone through with it. She would have seen the stones mixed in with the dirt along the edge of the slip, the holes and gaps and sharp edges just waiting to clip the wheels of her bike and send her tumbling. But she hadn't had time to think about it, so instead she barreled on down the hill and slammed directly into the shooter.

Later, Toni would remember thinking that everything happened at once, like a series of photographic negatives stacked one on top of the other. Slamming into the man full-on, sending him sprawling into the dirt. The ground rising up and smacking her. Winded, rolling downhill, trying to cover her head, but unable to tell whether she'd banged it on anything already, or even what part of her had hit the ground first.

The smell of hot dirt in her face.

Sun glaring in her eyes.

Pushing herself up, muscles screaming, head spinning. She had to run. She had to get to the van, the kids—

No.

That had been yesterday. It was light now, not dark. The kids were safe.

A voice in her head.

<Toni!>

Jack.

Toni stared across the bare earth at the man she had come to rescue, and the world stopped spinning. She had fallen off her bike and skidded halfway down the hill; the man she had hit lay crumpled on the ground.

His gun lay midway between them, smaller items scattered around it. Toni blinked. They looked like ... phials?

"Toni!"

"Jack!" She spun around and half-ran, half-skidded down the hill, her backpack smacking against her with every step.

Jack had turned away from de Jager and was moving toward her.

Behind him, Toni saw de Jager dash back to the car and pull out a gun. He leveled it at Jack's back.

"Jack, look out!" Even before the words left her lips, Jack was spinning around. Toni felt his shock like a blow as he saw the gun.

Then she felt the shots.

Toni gasped, and her hands flew to her chest. There was nothing there, just the same dirt-stained shirt as before. Then she saw Jack fall to his knees in front of her.

She ran to his side, knees buckling under her as she reached him. The phantom pain – *his* pain – still echoed in her body as Jack sank to the ground. She rolled him over, terrified by the thought of what she might see.

A metallic glint caught the light where she had expected to see blood. Something was sticking out of Jack's chest, and it wasn't bullets. Jack grunted as Toni pulled one of the darts out of his chest. It had a highlighter-yellow fletch and, under that, an empty syringe.

"Oh, god, Jack," Toni breathed. "It's a tranquilizer dart."

But it wasn't just one. It was three, bristling from Jack's heaving chest like monstrous flowers. Toni pulled the other two from her lover's body as fast as she could, but all three syringes were empty.

She'd been wrong. Whatever de Jager, or his boss, wanted out of Jack, it wasn't his death. This whole thing had been a trap meant to capture him alive. Render him unconscious, and helpless.

Jack's eyes were going unfocused, and Toni could tell he was losing consciousness as the drug kicked in. She mentally added up the quantity of tranquilizer that must have been in the three darts and felt ill. De Jager had shot Jack with enough tranquilizer to fell a huge animal – but for a human, that dose would be lethal. She held back a sob. De Jager's plan might fail, after all, but not for any reason she could have hoped.

She shook Jack's shoulder desperately as a shadow fell over her. "Jack, listen to me. Focus on my voice. The amount of tranquilizer you've got in your system – it's too much, it'll kill you. But your tiger might be able to deal with it. Jack, you have to transform. Trust me, you have to shift *now*."

Jack's eyelids flickered as he tried to fight the drug. His breath was slowing, as though his lungs were straining to work against a great pressure.

<*Toni, run!*> he urged her, but it was too late.

De Jager dragged Toni upright and pulled her around to face him. She recoiled as he leered at her, but he gripped her arm so tightly she couldn't move away.

"The mysterious Antonia Parker!" he crowed triumphantly. "Speaking of bonuses ... I can't think what my employer would do with you, sweetheart, but I'm sure one of his pet scientists will find you an interesting data point." He leaned in closer. "You and your niece and nephew."

Toni almost retched as de Jager drew her closer to his face.

"Don't you dare touch them!" she snarled. Silently, she shouted out to Jack to wake up, to fight the drugs, but there was only silence behind her. Even the long, dragging sound of Jack's breath had grown quiet.

Toni sobbed and threw her full weight at de Jager, hoping to knock him off balance. But he was ready for her, and threw her to the ground. Toni hit the dirt and lay there, stunned.

"I'd offer you the same deal I offered our friend here, but I get the feeling you'd suspect I wasn't being entirely truthful with you," de Jager said conversationally. They might have been exchanging small talk at an office party.

Toni's mind was racing. She glanced across to Jack. He hadn't moved, or shifted. Her heart lurched in her chest. Desperate, she held on to the connection she still felt between herself and the man she had fallen so quickly and deeply in love with. Focusing with all her energy, she sent her strength to Jack, willing him to fight the drugs that were coursing through his body – to be strong, to survive—

Toni's vision swam, and she never saw de Jager's boot swinging toward her. Pain burst along her side as he kicked her to the ground.

"I asked you a question, you damn freak! When I talk, you listen!"

Toni spat out a mouthful of dirt and glared up at de Jager. She had seen her sister and parents hiss and spit when they were enraged in cat form, their glossy coats puffing up to make them look bigger. In this moment, Toni understood what that must feel like. If she'd had hackles, they would have risen. If she'd had a tail, it would have been puffed up like a banner.

Instead, since she was a human, she made do with spitting all the profanities she could think of. She pushed herself onto her knees, ready to launch herself at de Jager, and then froze as he lifted the pistol and pointed it at her.

Behind the barrel of the gun, de Jager's mouth twisted into a greasy grin. "Not so fast, sweetheart. You just—"

<Don't you dare touch her!>

A black and orange flash rushed past Toni and smashed into de Jager. She had barely a moment to realize it was Jack before he sent gun and man flying in different directions with a single sweep of his powerful paws.

Toni was used to cat shifters, but a tiger was something totally different. She slowly stood up, taking in the scene in front of her. The tiger – Jack – was bigger than a normal tiger, reaching as high as Toni's shoulder even on all fours. Muscles bunching under his striped fur, he stood over de Jager, dwarfing the cowering man. A growl ripped from his throat as he padded forward.

"You wouldn't dare, you filthy brute," hissed de Jager. "You think I'm the only one who took on your contract? I might have tracked you down first, but if I turn up with my throat torn out you won't be able to move in these woods for our people. You and those fucking kids won't stand a chance."

Jack lowered his head. Toni heard his voice inside her mind, although he kept his golden eyes fixed firmly on de Jager.

<So, he's got allies, but none nearby, or he'd be threatening us with them to save his own hide.>

"Right," Toni agreed, not trusting herself to mindspeak without blasting the whole forest. Her adrenaline was spiking, filling her body with nervous energy. She looked back across the clearing at the sniper, who was beginning to groan softly.

So she hadn't killed him after all. She wasn't sure whether she was more relieved or annoyed that this meant he was still a problem.

She looked back at their would-be captor in time to see his eyes slide across the ground to his gun. It must have been ten feet away from him. Toni couldn't tell whether he was stupid, or desperate, enough to go for the weapon with four hundred kilograms of growling tiger standing over him, but she briskly walked over and picked it up anyway.

<You've got the other gun, too, don't you? I can smell it nearby.>

"Backpack," Toni confirmed. She didn't want to talk too much with de Jager listening in.

<Good. Don't bring it out unless it's absolutely necessary. This is all going to look crazy enough without ... hey!>

Jack punctuated this last, silent exclamation with a sharp growl. De Jager was slinking backwards toward the van. The vehicle wasn't likely to do much damage against Jack's supernatural bulk at this distance but if de Jager could get the engine running, he might escape. Toni pointed the gun at him.

"Stop moving!"

De Jager laughed, but Toni could see the whites around his eyes. Even if he was trying to hide it, he was afraid.

She knew that Jack was thinking the same thing; if she let her attention slip toward him, then she could almost start to smell de Jager's fear as well as see it, just as Jack could.

Interesting. She tucked that thought away for later.

De Jager licked his lips. "You know ... the deal I mentioned. Let's change it up a bit. I can tell my employer this whole contract is a dead end – nothing in it – I'll make sure they leave you alone..."

"And leave you free to hunt down other shifters?" Toni cried out. "Jack, stop him!"

De Jager lunged for the van door. Jack had started moving before Toni's warning left her lips. He leapt forward in one smooth movement and struck de Jager to the ground. He lay still.

"Bastard!" Toni shouted. "What kind of monsters does he think we are?"

<It was a trick> Jack reminded her gently.

Toni punched her hands into fists. To her surprise, there were tears in her eyes. "Did he think we would really take him up on that offer? Let him go free to attack other innocent shifters? I'd rather die!"

She felt warm fur under her hand. Jack was standing next to her; she realized she was shaking, and put out her arms to steady herself on his solid bulk. "I've done everything wrong this weekend. Even if he killed me, I couldn't let him hurt anyone else."

Her shakes turned into uncontrollable sobs. Everything that had happened that weekend seemed to wash over her in one unforgiving tide. Her failure to protect the twins. Her failure to contact her sister, to let anyone know what was going on. Even Jack had almost died because of her. Toni shut her eyes tight in a hopeless attempt to stem the flood of her tears and wrapped her arms around herself.

There was a soft, organic noise, Jack laid a human hand on her arm. She let him pull her toward him, into his warm embrace. He smelled like dirt, and sweat, all the tangible reminders of the tragedy they had only just avoided – but behind that, she sensed his own, personal smell, warm and animal and pure. She flung her arms around him and held on tight.

"I thought I had – I thought I was going to lose you," she mumbled into his chest. "When I saw de Jager shoot you – if I hadn't distracted you, if I hadn't made such a mess of things—"

"Don't regret anything you did today, Toni. You saved my life."

Jack gestured toward the shooter Toni had knocked from his perch, who moaning in a way that suggesting he wouldn't be getting up anytime soon.

"I should never have left the house without telling you what I was doing. If you hadn't found me, who knows where I would have woken up. Or not woken up."

He rubbed his shoulder absently, and Toni saw three small red marks where the shots had struck him. The puncture wounds looked old, almost completely healed over. She passed her own hand over them protectively. "That much tranquilizer should have been enough to kill you. I thought it had. I thought for sure that it knocked you out. What happened?"

Jack lifted her chin in both his hands, staring deep into her eyes. "You did, my love. My brave, beautiful Toni. I don't know how you did it, but everything was going dark, and then I heard your voice. You told me to be strong, and suddenly I was. I could still feel the drug pulling me down, but I could fight it. I could protect you."

He pressed his lips against Toni's in a lingering kiss.

"I love you, Toni. And I'll never stop protecting you." A smile flickered over his face. "So long as you promise to keep protecting me, too. I can't believe you ambushed the guy who was meant to ambush me! How did you find me?"

Toni felt a smile begin to grow on her own face. "You haven't figured it out yet? I might not be a proper shifter, Jack, but some shifter things I *definitely* understand." <*My love. My mate.*>

Toni saw the shock of happiness sweep across Jack's expression – and felt, too, the rush of joy that filled his heart. It filled her heart, too.

"I might not be able to shift, but I think today proves that I don't need to be a shifter to – to be worthwhile," she said, stumbling over the words.

"Toni, I—" He frowned, as though something had suddenly distracted his attention. Toni couldn't hear anything; then she let her senses slip sideways to piggyback on Jack's keener ones, and realized immediately what he had picked up on.

"Damn! I mean, obviously, good," she said, quickly correcting herself. She caught Jack's eye and blushed. "Look, you hear it too, right?"

"At least three vehicles," Jack confirmed. "Here comes the cavalry." Cavalry with sirens: for them, not de Jager and his accomplice.

Toni giggled. "This seems to be a habit with you. You do something heroic, but by the time someone else turns up all you're doing is standing around with no clothes on."

Jack swore and dove back to where his clothes lay in a shredded heap on the ground. His tiger was significantly bigger than his human form, and when he had transformed, the garments hadn't put up much of a fight.

He picked up the remains of his shirt and looked at them hopelessly.

"I seem to recall the last time this happened, the person who turned up was very understanding about my nakedness," he grumbled playfully, trying to match up split seams. "That's probably less likely to be the case today."

"Here," Toni said, fishing his trousers out of the pile. "These are ripped, but if you use my belt..."

Between them, they managed to get Jack looking slightly presentable before the police cars roared into the clearing. The cops had followed the same road de Jager had come in on, and his van was soon surrounded by flashing lights. Doors swung open and Toni braced herself to answer an onslaught of questions, but the first person to leap out of the back of a car and toward her was no police officer.

"Ellie!" Toni gasped, then looked beyond her sister to see a heavyset man struggling to extricate himself from the same car. "And Werther! What are you two doing here?"

Ellie flung her arms around her little sister. "I got your message last night – all your messages – and we came as fast as we could. We got to the twins just as the police arrived, and you know there is no way we were going to be left behind."

She squeezed Toni even more tightly, and Toni realized with a shock that her sister was crying. "Oh, god, Toni, I am so glad you're okay."

Werther finally managed to heave himself out of the car and walked sedately up to the trio. The reason for his trouble getting out of the passenger seat was clear – Lexi and Felix, both in human form, were clinging like monkeys to his back.

A police officer in what looked like a hastily-donned uniform ran up to belatedly flank the father and his children as they trampled over what was, after all, a crime scene.

"Toni," Werther said, reaching out to squeeze Toni's shoulder reassuringly.

Solid and reliable where his wife was fleet-footed and frenetic, Werther had the same sleepy green eyes in human form as he did as a Norwegian forest-cat shifter. He bore the weight of his twin children with apparent ease, and ignored the officer by his side the same way.

"And you must be Jack."

Toni watched the four closest members of her family silently look over the tall, muscular man – wearing little more than rags – who was standing protectively beside her, his arm still around her waist even as Ellie claimed her own hugs. A silent understanding passed through the group.

<Well,> Ellie said, smirking, as the twins grinned and Werther blinked calmly. <Welcome to the family, Jack.>

TWELVE
TONI

Evening was falling over the forest. Toni stood at Jack's living room window, watching the last rays of sunlight send brilliant orange and pink streaks across the sky. As the light finally disappeared, she marvelled at what a difference twenty-four hours could make. The evening before, she had been wracked with guilt and fear, her heart still thundering with terror from almost losing the twins; but now, she was at peace. De Jager's mysterious boss, the man who had sent him after Jack, might still be out there, but with Jack at her side, and her family behind her, Toni had no reason to be afraid.

<I know you're worrying> whispered Jack, standing behind her and wrapping his arms around her waist. <But – don't worry. We'll find whoever sent that monster to Silver Forest.>

"Yes, we will," Toni promised. "And with my family's shifter networks, we'll make sure every shifter in the country knows about the danger. No one will have to go through what happened to Lexi and Felix, ever again."

Outside the window, two small shadows darted to and fro across the wildflower-strewn yard. Ellie and Werther were sitting on the wide deck, her sleek black tail intertwined with his fluffy white one.

Jack kissed the side of Toni's neck, lingering there to nuzzle the sensitive skin behind her ear.

"I told you I would protect you. And that means your family, as well. My business has taken me all over the world, and if there's one thing I've learnt from it, it's how to deal with poachers. I have contacts on every continent who make it their life's work to track people who endanger innocent animals. It won't be difficult to find people who take the same interest in protecting innocent people."

"We can't," Toni said, her heart sinking. "It's bad enough that some humans know about shifters. How can we trust that anyone else we tell will keep the secret, keep it safe, and not exploit it like de Jager?"

"I know some trustworthy people," Jack reassured you. "And you don't need to worry about betraying the shifter secret. The folks I'm thinking of aren't human-shaped one hundred percent of the time."

Toni let herself relax back against Jack's broad chest, feeling his hard muscles against her back and shoulders. And lower down, something else was hard, as well. "That sounds like the sort of thing we can talk about more ... later. Maybe tomorrow?" She tipped her head back and caught Jack's questing mouth in a tender kiss.

She felt Jack's hesitation in her own heart even before he paused and pulled away. "Toni—"

She put her finger over his mouth. "Shh. I know exactly what you're going to say."

"I doubt that," he said promptly, his voice muffled by her fingers. Toni narrowed his eyes at him.

"Oh, I do. And I know *why* I know, as well. So do you. Ellie and Werther recognized it the moment they saw us. I don't know why it took me so long." She groaned self-consciously at the thought of how dense she had been. It had almost been as though she had been trying not to see the truth that was staring her in the face. As though she couldn't possibly believe she could be so lucky. "If I concentrate, I can feel what you feel, and not only your emotions. When I was tracking you down, before I even entered the forest I could smell the loamy soil under feel and hear the trees moving in the breeze around you. I thought it was just my shifter abilities asserting themselves at last, but it's more than that, isn't it?"

"It is," Jack breathed, holding himself still as though pinned in place by her fingers on his lips.

Toni stepped closer as Jack's affirmation washed over her. His eyes were thin rings of gold around deep black pupils, and she wanted nothing more than to sink into them, and leave the need for speech behind. But she knew this was something they both had to say aloud. She could feel the guilt still hiding in Jack's breast. And she had her own reasons.

"You're my mate. I didn't think that was possible. I might be from a shifter family, but I'm not a shifter, so I thought ... but it's true. From the moment I met you, I felt a connection to you, I trusted you. And the longer I spend with you, the more – the more I feel like myself. Like a better version of myself. Like I'm whole, for the first time in my life." She took a deep breath. "And that's why I need you to know. I don't mind that you kept your shifter self a secret from me at the riverbank yesterday."

Jack looked away, shame in his eyes. "I didn't know what to do. I knew you were my mate – but I could have dealt with it better. I could have talked to you, and not kept you away from the twins. If I hadn't been so selfish—"

"—Then maybe de Jager would have grabbed both of us as well as the twins. We already know he and his people were armed. He might have used the threat of hurting Lexi or Felix to blackmail you into giving yourself up without a fight. Or you might have had to shift at the campsite, in front of witnesses. He would have used your fear of discovery against you." She laid her hands on his shoulders. "Don't feel guilty, Jack. You had no way of knowing what de Jager was planning. And everything's turned out fine. We're all alive. De Jager is in custody. And we have each other." She leaned forward, nuzzling into his chest. "I never thought I would have a mate. I didn't think it was possible. And now I've got you. What more could I ask for?"

At last she felt the guilt lift from his heart. He wrapped his arms around her, holding her close against him. she stood on her tiptoes to press a kiss against his collarbone, and felt his hands drop down her back to clasp her waist.

"Toni..." he murmured.

"By the way," she interjected before he could say more, "I want to make it *very clear* that I personally regret *nothing* about our little interlude on the riverbank."

"No arguments here," Jack said, his voice rough. He slid one hand down farther, caressing the curve of her ass. "Though, I would definitely be open to hearing more about what, precisely, it is you don't regret. And I think I'm going to need a lot of detail."

Toni giggled into the soft fabric of Jack's shirt and gave

him a playful push toward the door. He grabbed her hand and pulled her after him.

They fell against each other as they hurried through to the staircase that led to the bedrooms. Through the wall-length windows, the forest looked like a dark ocean, the house a single island of light in the wilderness.

Toni squealed as Jack picked her up and leaped down the stairs. She wrapped her legs around him and braced herself as he landed on the floor at the bottom, surprisingly softly.

Jack's hands were running up and down her body, exploring and enjoying her curves as she knew he had longed to do since they had dispatched de Jager together. She let her feet slip to the ground and used that balance to press herself up against him.

She had felt his frustration as first her sister and brother-in-law, and then the police, had kept them with their interminable questions. But now, with the police gone and Toni's family considerately keeping to the other end of the house, he let his inhibitions go.

Still kissing her, Jack reached around to grab Toni's ass. He lifted her again without a grunt of effort. Toni gasped and wrapped her legs around his waist to steady herself, feeling the huge bulge at the front of his pants rubbing against her own throbbing center.

"Oh, Jack..." she moaned, and rubbed herself against him. "We're not even in the bedroom yet..."

She giggled as Jack theatrically rolled his eyes and, with exaggerated care, strode through the master bedroom door and closed it with a careful *click*. Just as she thought he was going to carry her to the super-king bed, he paused, and turned back to the wall.

"On second thoughts," he murmured, his breath hot in her ear, "let's not go to bed just yet."

"Don't you *dare*," growled Toni. "You can't bring me down here with your promises and then – oh...!"

Toni gasped as Jack leant her back against the wall, planting a line of rough kisses down her neck to her cleavage. And then lower. She steadied herself on his shoulders as he knelt in front of her, tearing her shirt from her body as he went. Every inch of skin he uncovered, he teased with his mouth and his hands, until Toni was quivering with desire.

When he got to her trousers he took his time over the fastenings. Toni could feel his fingers through the heavy fabric of her jeans, working tantalisingly slowly. She moaned and pushed herself toward him, and he understood immediately, cupping her mound in the palm of his hand. He pressed upwards against her, the heat and pressure of his hand bringing Toni's pleasure to an exquisite point. She ground against his hand. The seams of her jeans, caught between her flesh and his, send jolts of white-hot pleasure through her as she rolled over them. Toni flung her head back, eyes staring blindly at the wall and plaster ceiling—

Then the rough, impersonal denim was replaced by hot flesh. Jack pulled her jeans down to her ankles and slid two fingers into her, the sudden intrusion into her slick folds making Toni almost scream with liquid lust. She kicked off her trousers and almost collapsed as Jack's curled his fingers inside her and brushed against her g-spot. She struck out blindly with her hands and grabbed on to his hair and one shoulder, steadying herself before her legs gave out and she fell on top of him.

Jack grinned up at her. He slid his free hand slowly up her

leg, leaving her skin goosebumped in its wake. Then he began to stand up, still maddeningly slowly, still gently stroking inside her.

Toni's breathing was ragged. She was close, so close – but she didn't want to come before he was inside her. She wanted to feel his long, thick cock thrusting into her, deeper and deeper, grounding her and pushing her over the edge at the same time.

<What was that?> whispered a teasing voice inside her head. Toni narrowed her eyes.

<You heard me> she replied.

With that he rose up against her, fumbling at his own clothes. First his shirt and then his pants joined hers on the floor, thrown off and as quickly forgotten. Then he was on her, both hands on her hips, pinning her to the wall. He shifted his grip down and back behind her, lifting her against him again. This time, there was no fabric separating their bodies. His skin was hot against hers, and she could feel the rock-hard head of his cock pressing against her, between her legs, as he lowered her onto his thick length. Her slick folds parted willingly for him and she moaned as he entered her.

Jack groaned into Toni's hair as he plunged deep inside her, burying his cock to its full length on the first smooth thrust. He pulled her away from the wall and she wrapped her legs around his waist, gasping as the motion shifted his cock inside her.

<Hmm. Is this right? I'm still not quite sure what you were after,> he teased, steadying her hips with his hands. Toni grabbed his head with both hands and kissed him, running her tongue along his lower lip.

"I'm not going to answer that," she whispered back, her

voice catching as he lifted her hips and then lowered them again, pumping his cock in and out of her. "You're going to have to ... oh-h..."

"I think I have my answer," he murmured wickedly, his tongue flicking out to taste her skin as he nuzzled her neck. "Though perhaps I should make you elaborate on it?"

He put one hand out to lean on the wall behind Toni, his other still holding her ass firmly in place as he thrust his thick cock into her, harder and harder, deeper and deeper until Toni's whole world was whittled down to the pleasure of touch, the ever-larger waves of hot desire that were flooding her body.

When her orgasm came it burst out of her in a scream, every muscle in her body straining for pleasure. Toni clamped her legs tight around Jack's body, grinding herself against his cock to make the exquisite moment last as long as possible. Her whole body was slick with sweat, and it was only Jack's strong hands that kept her held tightly against him. She felt him come just as she had crested her own orgasm, and the feeling of his cock twitching inside her brought her to another peak. As the last throbbing echoes of her orgasm faded away, so did the last of her energy, and she let herself relax utterly on her lover's strong, muscular body.

Still panting with exertion, Jack wrapped his arms around her, holding her as gently as though he was afraid she would break, or just disappear. She planted a tiny kiss on his shoulder where her head had fallen. "I'm not going anywhere," she murmured.

"Hmm?"

"Mmm."

There was a moment's silence. Toni could almost feel

Jack's mind ticking over, even without the mate bond. She giggled into his shoulder.

"What's so funny?"

"Go on, say it."

"Say what?"

Toni drew lazy spirals on Jack's back with her fingertips. "Say, 'Oh, you don't want to go to bed, then?'" she said, mimicking the impending joke she had sensed rising to the surface of Jack's mind.

Jack sighed, and walked them both over to the huge bed. He laid Toni down on the coverlet, staring sadly into her eyes. "This is going to be a problem. I'm going to have to start thinking more carefully about my jokes."

They lay on the bed together, sweat cooling on their entwined bodies. Toni had never felt so contented – so safe. The world, for the first time in a long time, seemed to offer adventure rather than worry and frustration. And it was no longer something that she would have to face alone.

She stared up at Jack's face, blissful and contented in repose. But his eyes were bright, a gleaming gold in the darkened room. "I know what you're thinking," she teased.

He looked down at her and she almost lost herself again in those deep, hot pools. "Well?" he prompted her after a minute. "You were saying...?"

Ah. Maybe not *almost*, then. She blushed. "Well, I know what you're thinking *now*, now. But a minute ago—"

"Five minutes ago—"

Toni laughed indignantly and rolled on top of her lover,

pinning his arms to the mattress with her knees. "A minute ago, you were thinking – this is a happy ending. The happiest ending."

Jack raised his eyebrows. "Weren't you thinking the same thing?"

"No. And what's more, you're wrong." She leant down, her breasts brushing against his broad chest, her face only inches from his. "This isn't the *end* of anything. It's the beginning. The beginning of *us*. Of happiness, of adventures – of our life together."

"Together. I like the sound of that," Jack murmured, his eyelids flickering against Toni's cheek. "Almost as much as I love you."

With that settled, they both thought very hard about what the best way to commemorate this new beginning might be. And after they had decided the best way to mark the occasion – and marked it a few more times – they fell asleep.

Outside the window, a silvery new moon cast its light over Jack and Toni's forest, and the world in which they would spend their lives together. Not a perfect world, not a safe one – but a world they could face, together.

CPSIA information can be obtained
at www.ICGtesting.com
Printed in the USA
LVHW041723080119
603164LV00002B/259/P

9 781520 243917